DEATH ABOARD SHIP

Inside the cabin, Micky the Slob was reclining on a bunk, his porcine eyes half closed, staring at the door. Sticking out of the neck of an empty beer barrel, looking like a fat cigarette, was a tube of nitroglycerine. It was enough to destroy the ship.

A crackling came from the loud-speaker, built into the ceiling. "Glad you've been sensible so far, Micky," the voice said.

Micky muttered, "That's Gideon."

A little frothy saliva gathered at the corners of his mouth.

He bent down and picked up the bomb.

J.J. MARRIC MYSTERIES

Time passes quickly . . . As *DAY* blends with *NIGHT* and *WEEK* flies into *MONTH*, Gideon must fit together the pieces of death and destruction before time runs out!

GIDEON'S DAY   (2721, $3.95)
The mysterious death of a young police detective is only the beginning of a bizarre series of events which end in the fatal knifing of a seven-year-old girl. But for Commander George Gideon of New Scotland Yard, it is all in a day's work!

GIDEON'S MONTH   (2766, $3.95)
A smudged page on his calendar, Gideon's month is blackened by brazen and bizarre offenses ranging from mischief to murder. Gideon must put a halt to the sinister events which involve the corruption of children and a homicidal housekeeper, before the city drowns in blood!

GIDEON'S NIGHT   (2734, $3.50)
When an unusually virulent pair of psychopaths leaves behind a trail of pain, grief, and blood, Gideon once again is on the move. This time the terror all at once comes to a head and he must stop the deadly duel that is victimizing young women and children—in only one night!

GIDEON'S WEEK   (2722, $3.95)
When battered wife Ruby Benson set up her killer husband for capture by the cops, she never considered the possibility of his escape. Now Commander George Gideon of Scotland Yard must save Ruby from the vengeance of her sadistic spouse . . . or die trying!

EDGAR AWARD WINNER

J·J·MARRIC
Gideon's Staff

ZEBRA BOOKS
KENSINGTON PUBLISHING CORP.

ZEBRA BOOKS

are published by

Kensington Publishing Corp.
475 Park Avenue South
New York, NY 10016

First Zebra Books printing: October, 1989

Printed in the United States of America

CONTENTS

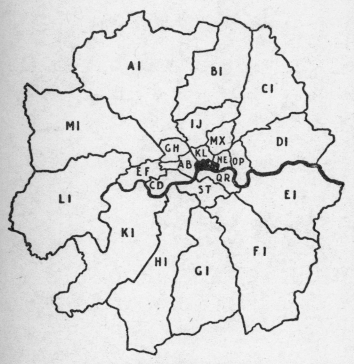

SKETCH MAP OF GIDEON'S TERRITORY

The map conforms only approximately to the boundaries of the
Metropolitan and City Police Forces and the divisional reference
letters do not coincide with the real London divisional letters or
boundaries

1

AXE

"The trouble with criminals is that they don't learn their job," Keith Ryman said. There was a faintly sardonic smile on his handsome face as he stood by the bar in his flat, martini in hand. The only other man present looked at him as if warily.

"You'd better not say that to Charlie Daw."

"Forget Daw, he's small beer," Ryman said. "I don't mean they're not good craftsmen. If you get the right man he can open a safe or pick a lock as well as a mechanic can fit a carburettor. The craftsmen are all right, but no one studies crime like men study big business or the professions," asserted Ryman, and smoothed down his fair, curly hair; now he was smiling broadly. "I think I could make a real go of it, Rab."

"If anyone could, you could," Stone said. He was a smaller man, rather sallow, and his well-tailored suit and spotted red and white tie and socks fell just short of being flashy as his manner was just short of being sycophantic.

"No doubt I could," Ryman agreed, nodding his head as at a well-deserved compliment. "This is the time to begin, too."

"Why's that?" asked Stone.

"Don't you ever keep your ears open?"

"Try me."

"In the Regal bar last night there were two Scotland Yard men, cribbing like hell because they'd got to go back on duty. Remember?"

Stone's eyes lit up with recollection.

"That's right. There were—and moaning like stink because the Yard's short-handed. One of them said they really need three men for every two they've got."

Ryman sipped his drink, contemplated his crony, and although he tried hard to restrain it, excitement made his eyes shine, and pitched his voice a key higher.

"That's it," he assented. "The police are short-handed, and they don't say too much about it because it might encourage the crooked fraternity to put in overtime. They play it down all right, but a really smart man could find a way to take advantage of this situation, Rab. I think I'm the man."

"You certainly get ideas," Stone said. "Anything in mind already?"

"Yes,' Ryman answered, softly. "We've got to get them on one foot, Rabbie, put 'em off balance. That's the strategy, all I've got to work out are the tactics. Are you in on this?"

"Believe me I'm in," Stone assured him, eagerly. "I've got the right contacts, too. We'll make the best team in London." His excitement was less controlled than Ryman's. "How about another drink, to close the deal?"

Ryman nodded, and Stone went to the other side of the bar to mix the drinks. Ryman said very little after that, but his thoughts were furiously active. He had real ability and a good mind, but a streak of weakness and a bigger one of cruelty had warped his attitude towards living. He made most of his money by his wits,

10

often at cards, and the polish of a minor public school helped him with that and also served him well socially.

Now he began to see himself as a man of genius, the only one with the wit to take advantage of a situation, and Stone fed his self-esteem with great skill.

Although George Gideon, Commander of the Criminal Investigation Department at New Scotland Yard, was also aware of the problem of manpower in the Force, he was not thinking of it the next morning. He was thinking about Sir Reginald Scott-Marle, the Commissioner. Scott-Marle was a somewhat remote person even to the other Chiefs at the Yard. He took the chair at the weekly conferences of assistant commissioners and heads of departments, but appeared to hold the reins at Scotland Yard very lightly. That did not mean ineffectively. In the course of nearly thirty years' service, Gideon had known several commissioners, and none had done a sounder or more balanced job than Scott-Marle. He had the trick or the gift of getting the best out of most officers, and of finding the right man for the various key posts at the Yard.

Nevertheless, Gideon was conscious of an invisible barrier between him and the Commissioner, and did not see how it could be avoided. Sir Reginald Scott-Marle had been born with a golden spoon in his mouth, came from a long line in a family with ducal forbears and, before being appointed to this job, had held two key Colonial posts. George Gideon had been born to an obscure West London couple, had neither reason nor desire to think back beyond his grandparents, and in a sardonic mood would call himself 'an old London Elementarian'. In fact he had left school at fourteen. The barrier seemed more than social; it was in outlook, in understanding of the same people and situations, and

11

in daily living. When Gideon got home he liked to take his coat off and do some decorating or carpentry, almost any odd job about the house except washing-up. Scott-Marle would put on a smoking-jacket, burrow in Greek mythology, and even in those days be waited on by butler, footman and maids. Gideon knew that, for he had twice been to see his Chief in the evening, on urgent matters concerning the treatment of suspects who had diplomatic immunity. Gideon also knew the Commissioner's wife slightly. She was twenty years younger than Scott-Marle, and quite a beautiful woman.

One of the troubles with which Gideon had grown up at Scotland yard was the preponderance of the uniformed and civil service men in the Force over the members of the Criminal Investigation Department. He found it increasingly difficult to be patient with some of the other departments and occasionally was annoyed because, combined, they carried so much weight. Scott-Marle did not appear to take sides, but sometimes Gideon thought that his years as a Colonial administrator had given him above-average understanding of the problems of the CID. In these days, with the crime rate fluctuating from year to year, but usually becoming higher, the Department's problems were increasing alarmingly.

A major one was that of getting suitable recruits. Gideon, who had the perhaps quaint idea that this chief job was to direct the investigation side of the Department, found himself increasingly involved in such matters as the training of uniformed men and recruiting for the Metropolitan Police as a whole.

On the morning of the first conference in the month of May, Gideon was in his office, going over the report of the night's events and the morning's mail, with a Chief Inspector whom he did not much like or respect. His regular aide was down with influenza, his second choice was taking part of his holiday before the summer rush of the men with young families, and this particular CI, Riddell, was not used to Gideon's likes and dislikes; he was a bit prosy, and had far too high an opinion of himself.

He was sitting at one side of Gideon's big desk, Gideon at the other. The pile of reports, mountainous at the beginning of this session, was reduced to the last half-inch. Most mornings Gideon saw the superintendents and inspectors handling the different cases, but the conference was due to start at ten, it was already to a quarter to, and he had to leave more than he liked to Riddell.

He glanced at the next report which read:

As instructed, I proceeded with a detective officer to 51 Canning Street, SW3, to prefer a charge of breaking and entering against Eric Thomas Jones. On arrival, I was informed that Jones had not been home all night. On request I was permitted by Mrs. Jones to search the premises, and came to the conclusion that Jones had not spent the night there. His wife stated that she could give no information as to his whereabouts.

Gideon felt as if he wanted to growl more fiercely with each sentence. The report was signed by a Detective Sergeant Worth, whom he knew comparatively slightly.

"My God!" he exclaimed. "Does Worth always write like this?"

"What's the matter with the report?" asked Riddell. "Quite straightforward, isn't it?"

Gideon made himself say: "I'm glad you can find some merit in it. Why wasn't Jones watched? He was

13

here, in our hands, yesterday afternoon. How'd we come to lose him?"

"There was no instruction about having him followed," answered Riddell. He showed no sign of resentment, and probably did not notice the undertone of exasperation in Gideon's voice. He probably regarded Worth's piece of witness-box prose as a model report.

"No instruction," Gideon echoed, and pushed his chair back. "You knew we were going to pick him up, didn't you? You knew——"

"*I* wasn't in charge of the case, that was Bell's job. If Bell had wanted Jones followed, presumably he would have given the instructions."

"Go and get Bell," ordered Gideon.

Riddell now looked annoyed, but he pushed his chair back and got up, going out without a word. In his shirt sleeves and with his collar loose, Gideon stood up, went to the window overlooking the Embankment, and fastened his collar and knotted his tie. The morning was pleasantly warm, the river looked bright, the red buses made vivid splashes of colour on Westminster Bridge; a beautiful morning.

"*Instruction*," breathed Gideon.

He was glad of the three minutes' respite, so as to get a firmer hold on himself. It was useless to lose his temper with Riddell, the man simply hadn't the ability this job required. He thought that Bell had, Bell was next in line—but if he'd fallen down on a simple job, he must be slipping. The conference would start in less than ten minutes, so there was really no time to go into details; that filled Gideon with self-annoyance, he ought not to have allowed himself to be goaded into sending for Bell.

The door swung open, and Riddell and Bell came in. They made quite a contrast, and if looks were everything, Riddell was the better man. He was handsome in a heavy-jowled way, dressed more like a stockbroker than a Chief Inspector of the CID, and looked immaculate; his brown eyes were alert-looking and his hair was either dyed or of very healthy pigmentation. Bell was a shorter, plumper man, with untidy grey hair, and his trousers always needed pressing. He liked to smoke a pipe, and he had grey eyes which twinkled; a fatherly looking chap, Gideon always thought, with a good, reflective mind. Obviously Riddell had 'warned' Bell that Gideon was on the warpath, and there was no twinkle now; he was over-formal.

"Good morning, Commander."

"Why the hell didn't you have Jones followed from here yesterday? You knew we'd want him before long, and that he'd slipped away before. We might be looking for him for months."

"Had three men available and four jobs to do," Bell answered quietly, "and I thought it was better to take a risk with Jones than slip up on the other jobs." He had an even, matter-of-fact way of speaking.

Gideon thought: 'He's right, and I'm the one who's slipping.' He rubbed the end of his heavy chin, and saw Riddell with a smug I-told-you-so look on his smooth face. "You had two chaps on the Morrison job and one after the old woman, but what about the two who finished the work out at Walton?"

"Sent 'em home, they'd been out two nights in a row."

"So it boils down to not having enough men," Gideon said heavily. "I'm going along to the conference this very minute, I'll see if I can dig something out of the powers that be. Thanks, Bell. Let me know when you pick Jones up. What's this chap Worth like?"

"Means well," answered Bell.

"Oh, Gawd,' breathed Gideon, and looked at Riddell. "I'll take a call about that Scottish job and another from Paris, keep everything else away from me while I'm with the big noise, will you?"

"Yes, Commander."

Gideon saw Bell open the door for him, and stepped into the passage. Bell closed the door and followed him, but didn't speak. They reached the corner, Bell to go down in the lift, Gideon to walk down one flight of stairs and then across to the other building.

"Joe," said Gideon, "do you ever long for the quiet life?"

"Long for it? I sigh for it."

"I mean, really somnolent, like sitting-in for me when I'm not in the office."

"Cheer up, Race will soon be back," Bell said. Race was Gideon's chief aide. "And there'll never be another one like Lemaitre. You ought to have kept him away from the Divisions. Voracious, those Divisions are."

"Meaning, you'd rather stay where you are?"

"Depends. Is it worth another hundred a year?"

"Shouldn't think so, but it might be," said Gideon. "Seriously, how'd you feel about it?"

"Would jump at the chance of being with you," Joe Bell answered, and then the lift arrived. "That's if anyone has the privilege in future. You're going to be late, and I've been told that unpunctuality doesn't please his nibs."

"He's not so bad," said Gideon.

Yet he hurried, down the stairs and along the wide passage which linked the two buildings, his long stride covering a lot of ground. He was big and massive, slightly round-shouldered because of his height, with iron-grey hair which was swept straight back from a broad forehead. His eyes were the same colour as his hair, and he did not yet wear glasses. He had a hardy-

16

looking skin, neither coarse nor fine, big but well-shaped hands and feet. He gave the impression of jousting an invisible adversary as he went along, and was quite aware that several men he passed, some CID and some on the civilian staff, turned and looked at him, and afterwards whispered about him.

The conference-room door was closed, and an 'engaged' sign was pinned to it. He thrust the door open and stepped in. There was a small ante-room, another open door, and beyond this a long, narrow table; it was like a company boardroom in a prosperous business. The chairs were padded and massive, the table glowed with polish, and the walls were panelled in medium-brown oak. 'They find the money for this,' Gideon thought. Scott-Marle was talking in his rather clipped way, hardly moving his lips. The other Commanders, his own Assistant Commissioner, the other ACs, the secretary, and the chief of the Solicitor's office were there, as well as the Public Relations Officer. It was a group exclusively of men, mostly grey-haired, bald or balding, sitting a little self-consciously, as always at the beginning of a meeting like this.

Scott-Marle had a cold fish approach.

There was one vacant chair, half way along one side. Gideon went to it. Scott-Marle did not pause to acknowledge his arrival, but continued quietly:

". . . and so we have to accept the fact that the decreased budget of fifty thousand pounds is the worst we need expect this year, although I've been told that the Treasury is reluctant to admit that. It's useless to ask for more, so we shall have to manage. Wherever possible we must make economies, of course, and that is one of the tasks I want to talk about. How long will it take before each department can examine its methods and recommend operative economies? If we don't do something, we shall find them forced upon us, and it would be unwise to have to make cuts under pressure."

He stopped.

The grey-haired male stenographer taking notes stopped almost at the same instant.

The Assistant Commissioner for the Uniformed Branch was the first to speak.

"We keep everything under constant review, and know just where economics can be made, if essential. I don't approve of them, of course, but as it's part of the general Government economy campaign, we will have to do it." He finished, smoothing a bald head with a great show of virtue, and sat a little more relaxed. The AC for Traffic said much the same thing, but grumbled more; he could have recommendations ready in a week.

Arthurson, of Research, said rather gruffly:

"If I chop off a fiver, it will mean I get less done. Don't they see that this is the one thing we can't afford to economise on?"

"I agree about that," put in the Uniformed Branch AC. "We need more, not less, uniformed police on the beat, I'm sure everyone will agree with that. However, if it is in the national interest, we'll have to do it."

Most of the others had a little say; none of them was satisfied, those who were not self-righteous in their willingness to make a sacrifice were glumly resigned to the inevitable.

Gideon was at a disadvantage too, and it was his own fault. He liked to sit next to Hugh Rogerson, the Assistant Commissioner for Crime, so that they could exchange notes and whispers, but Rogerson was hemmed in by Traffic and Research. He was worried about Rogerson, in any case; he knew that the older man was not well, and was finding it more and more difficult to cope.

Inevitably, the Commissioner looked at him.

"What can you promise us, Mr. Rogerson?"

Rogerson shrugged.

"Nothing, I should think." He had a droll way and a sense of humour which Gideon liked; he got along extremely well with his AC and hoped that his health would not force his resignation. He leaned forward and looked sideways along the table at Gideon. "Can we pare off a bit, Gideon?"

"It isn't yet a question of whether we can or we can't, we shall have to," declared Scott-Marle, "but the immediate question is how long will it be before you can assess the situation, and give estimates on the amount of economy you can achieve?"

Rogerson shrugged.

"Say a couple of weeks," he said. "Might be three."

Gideon was sitting very still, back firm against his chair, big hands clasped on the table, staring at an inkstand. His reflection showed indistinctly in the high polish; so did that of the other men, and of pads and pencils. He was the only one present who hadn't yet spoken, was fuming inwardly, and hoped that he did not show it; he had shown his feelings too much this morning already, his mood was unreliable.

"Have you any comment, Gideon?" Scott-Marle asked.

Now everyone was watching or waiting for Gideon to speak.

"Plenty I could say, but I don't see that it would do any good," he said, in his deep voice; he was normally a slow-speaking man, but now he spoke almost briskly.

Scott-Marle said: "I'd be interested to hear what it is."

So he was going to be forced into possible comment, Gideon realised; but he still hesitated. He knew exactly what he would like to say, but was doubtful whether it would serve the slightest useful purpose, and there was no point in rubbing Scott-Marle or any of the others up the wrong way. He unclasped his hands and slid his right hand into his pocket, to smooth the big bowl of the pipe he kept there, but seldom smoked. Someone coughed.

"Let's have it, George," urged Rogerson, quite unexpectedly; he was always the one most likely to unfreeze the conference atmosphere.

Gideon took out his pipe.

"Well," he said, with great deliberation, "our department alone wants another two hundred and fifty men, at least twenty per cent more floor space than we've got, and every man-jack in it ought to get a twenty per cent rise. The starting salaries ought to be increased, too. I dare say we could manage on an extra half a million." He gave a quick grin, which made him look surprisingly youthful, and was glad that he could speak without the slightest outward sign of exasperation; no one could be more dispassionate than he sounded. "I know what I'd do it I had my way. I'd tell the Home Office that fifty thousand pounds off was impossible. I'd ask them to have a look at the realities of life. I don't know about anyone else. I can only talk about my department, and my department's probably the one most affected by those realities. Crime is going up again. It's practically back to where it was in the bad days just after the war, and it's likely to get worse before it gets better. I don't think it'll get better unless we can put on extra men, and even if we get the money, it's going to be a hell of a job training them. I'd tell the Home Office that they can get ready for the biggest crime wave London's had since 1939, and as things stand now there isn't a thing we can do about it. If our cash is cut, the situation will get worse. I'm serious," he added, and looked straight into Scott-Marle's pale blue eyes. "I think the Government and the public ought to be warned what we're up against, then whatever happens we'll be able to say we told you so. One thing's certain, too; if we have to pare off a penny in my department, we'll have our noses rubbed in the dust pretty soon. We've got these new vice laws, we've got—oh, what the hell, we all know that the work's doubled in ten years, don't we? Let's ask a question and make someone answer: do we want to stop crime, or don't we? If we do, then what tools are we going to be given to stop it? If we go on as we are, we're going to be bloody near helpless."

He stopped, had to do something and put the empty pipe to his lips. The Commissioner showed no reaction as he looked round the big table. For a few moments, no one spoke. Then one man said in a rather high-pitched voice:

"I think that's an unnecessarily gloomy view of the situation, Commissioner. We aren't the only Force which has had to economise. The Armed Services had been very severely reduced in number, but there is no reason to assume that the efficiency has been affected adversely." The word 'efficiency' was the barb: Gidgeon felt it even before it was delivered, but he was never troubled by inter-departmental slanging matches which occasionally cropped up. "In my considered view, the Uniformed Branch has greater reason to complain about understaffing, but the Assistant Commissioner concerned hasn't raised that issue at this meeting."

That AC never raised an issue.

The invitation to argue on the importance of one department against another did not snare Gideon. So far, no one had agreed with him. Rogerson might—unless he thought that enough had been said already.

21

Rogerson was a man who liked peace; if he had a weakness, it was that he would not fight for his department.

"I quite see the point about the Armed Services," remarked a District Commissioner who would not have made that contribution unless he felt sure that the Chairman was unimpressed by Gideon.

Gideon said, very mildly: "There's one big difference, isn't there?"

"What?" asked a man he couldn't see.

"The Armed Services aren't fighting a war," Gideon said. "We are. I don't have to tell anyone here that we never stop, but I don't suppose you'll see it my way, that's why I didn't chime in before. Since you ask me, Commissioner, I should have to resist any attempt to force economies on the Criminal Investigation Department, because I couldn't do my job if they were forced on me."

He sensed the general disagreement, and was now certain that no one would back him up. He remembered little Eric Jones, somewhere on the run when he should have been awaiting the first magistrate's court hearing. He thought of the fact that he had an incompetent like Riddell with him, or else the need to take a first-class detective, such as Bell off the job he was most suited for. He felt angry against people and circumstances which he could only vaguely comprehend; there was really no one to fight. If we could talk this to the Home Secretary, then perhaps it might make some impression; as it was, this would not even get the conference support.

He must not show his feelings too strongly, but he was suddenly overwhelmed with the need to show the Commissioner just how deeply he felt. So he added quietly:

"And if I couldn't do the job, I'd rather not have it. I'd rather be back on the cab rank, then I would know that if I were assigned to a a case, I could see it through. I wouldn't have the feeling that I often get now—frustration after frustration, job after job falling down. This very morning I learned of a dangerous criminal we missed because we had four jobs to do and three men to do it with, and the Divisions are just as badly off."

At least he had caused a sensation; he could tell that by the way most of those on the other side of the table were looking at him; by the sharp intake of breath in the man on his right; by the way Rogerson leaned forward and stared at him, unbelievingly.

The Commissioner asked, as if coldly:

"Are you serious about that, Gideon?"

2

ANSWER

Gideon thought: 'Now I've done it.' He thought: 'He's quite capable of taking me up on it, too.' He had a moment of anxiety, and then saw a new line of approach, so emphatic that it surprised him. He wanted to say: 'Yes, sir, I am serious, never been more serious in my life. What the hells' the use of working like I work if they're going to sabotage it by being mean as muck?'

The thoughts flashed through his mind while everyone waited; but a moment or two would not matter, he was always inclined to deliberate before he spoke, and the longer the pause this time, the more they would realise that he meant whatever he said.

There was utter silence round the table.

"Yes," answered Gideon, at last. "Dead serious, Commissioner."

Rogerson was stung to saying: "Now, George——" and broke off.

There was another period of silence, and Gideon's mind was moving very swiftly; only those who knew him well realised that he had such mental agility. At least two of the District Commanders were thinking that if he resigned, they might get his job. One was eager, almost greedy for it; the other would shy away. The Assistant Commissioners were probably sympathising with Rogerson for having such a problem in his department, too. Then quite unexpectedly little Forbes, of Research, grinned across the table at Gideon, and said:

"Don't know that I would go that far, but I'm with you in principle, George. We ought to kick against this, and find a way to make the Home Office realise that they're really cutting the supply lines of a military operation." He turned to Scott-Marle, with him he was on equal terms in nearly every way, for he was Harrow and Oxford. "Why don't you send a note back, saying that it can't be done?"

"But it *must* be done," one of the ACs declared, and actually thumped the table.

Gideon did not hear everything that was said in the next few minutes. He watched the Commissioner, almost furtively, wondering uneasily what would be the outcome. He did not yet regret his answer, but his mind was beginning to run on the possible consequences. If the Commissioner wished, he could force his resignation. That would mean the loss of four hundred pounds a year and a great deal of prestige. No one would believe that he stepped down willingly; it would be assumed that he had been pushed. That wouldn't be much fun.

And there was Kate; and home.

Gideon was uneasy because the Commissioner gave no clear idea of what he was thinking.

Two other men came down on Gideon's side after all, the Research man had won them over, but no one committed himself to such vehemence as Gideon.

"Thank you, gentlemen," the Commissioner said, into a lull. "We will take it, then, that each department will advise the Secretary within two weeks what economies if any can be made, and how best they can be effected without causing a deterioration in the department's efficiency." He paused, and Gideon's heart sank fast. "If any department feels convinced that any economy is impossible without deterioration, that will be stated on the report of course." That was a little better, almost a concession. Then the Commissioner looked straight at Gideon. "If any department is able to cite specific instances of inefficiency or failure due to shortage of staff, I hope they will be added."

He paused.

'Fair enough,' Gideon thought, a little ruefully. 'Eric Jones, you might be worth more than you think.'

"The next item on the agenda concerns the Bank Holiday weekend traffic problems, and there is a report on the result of the temporary arrangements made last Easter," said the Commissioner.

Gideon did not pay much attention to the traffic problems, although most of what he heard would stay in his mind and if necessary he would be able to quote it at any time during the next week or two. He was busy going back over the events of the last few weeks, and trying to think of cases which had fallen on their face because of manpower shortage. There were dozens; but it would not always be possible to trace the cause back directly. He knew it, any practical man knew, but when it became a matter of putting the cases down in black and white, it wasn't going to be easy. He built up two cases and then imagined what a defending counsel would make of them.

Hay.

Several other items on the agenda had little direct association with the CID, even though most of the departments overlapped. He joined in the discussion several times, behaving as if the major issue had not been forced, but he suspected that his challenge was on everyone's mind when, a little after twelve-thirty, the conference broke up. By then, he had thought of many other things that he would have liked to say, but he could not open the subject again.

The Commissioner was summoned hastily, and had only a chance to give a general, "Good-day, gentlemen," before being ushered out.

The Research chief spoke almost as the door closed:

"Did the best I could for you, George, but now you've got your hands full."

"Rather spend my time checking the harmful effects of manpower shortage than seeing how we can save a penny here and tuppence there," Gideon retorted.

"Yes, I suppose so."

"The thing you don't seem to understand," said Uniform, "is that this is an edict from the Home Office, which they've had from the Treasury. It's a directive."

"Might just as well accept it, instead of kicking," said Traffic. "God knows I'm bitter enough about lack of manpower, but it's no us cutting off my nose to spite my face."

"George," asked a District Commander, "would you really resign?"

Gideon gave a slow, ruminative smile, and answered:

"Have a job not to now, wouldn't I? But it would be worth it if we can make the Old Man see that this particular directive wants putting you-know-where."

He took the first opportunity to leave, and was glad that only Research went with him.

"Stick to your guns, George," he urged. "Someone has to."

"I know, I'll make a nice Roman holiday," Gideon said.

He went back to his office, opened the door, expected to find Riddell at the desk opposite his own, a

27

smaller desk with four telephones, but Riddell was not there; nor was the sergeant. Gideon had told Riddell and everyone who worked here with him that the office must never be empty during the day; but here it was, and suddenly two telephones began to ring at once. He snatched at the one on his desk.

"Gideon."

"Bell here," said Chief Inspector Bell. "I've got some good news for you."

The other bell kept ringing, at Riddell's desk.

Gideon grunted.

"Don't sound so pleased," protested Bell. "We've got Eric Jones, so it only made twelve hours' difference. Picked him up at his sister's place, in Poplar."

Gideon made himself sound hearty.

"Nice work, Joe, keep it up. Can't stop now, I've two or three things to do." He put the receiver down with a bang and strode across to the other desk, snatched that receiver up, and barked: "Gideon." There was a little gasp, and then a woman said:

"Oh, I'm so sorry. I thought my husband would be there."

"Who is that?"

"I'm Mrs. Riddell."

Gideon grunted: "No, he's——" and then the door opened and Riddell came in. "Here he is." He held out the receiver. "Your wife." Riddell took the receiver, looked at him a little uncertainly, and then said: "Hullo, dear, I'd just been out of the office for a moment." He held the telephone cable away from a corner of the desk so that he could go and sit down, listening all the time. He must have listened for five minutes, with only an occasional comment. Then he said: "Yes, I don't know of anything that will keep me later than six, I'll be there on time . . . Goodbye dear." He rang off. "Got some friends coming in tonight," he told Gideon. "My wife always gets into a panic in case something crops up to make me late. I told her that while I was in this office she needn't worry, it's only when you're on the investigation staff that you can't call your life your own."

Gideon grunted.

He did not enjoy the rest of the day. It was useless to keep railing at Riddell, but the man irritated him far too much. There was no time to give his mind to the problem that he had set himself, but whenever he managed an odd thought about it the more difficult the task appeared. It was a variation on a familiar theme; everyone knew that manpower shortage was responsible for many failures to solve crimes from murder downwards, just as the Yard often knew who had committed a certain crime; getting the evidence to satisfy a court was as difficult as getting more staff.

"What I want is a few hours to think about it," he told himself. "Kate's in for a quiet night." His wife was wont to complain that when in the middle of a puzzling or worrying case, he was capable of sitting for hours staring into space, fiddling with his pipe, almost forgetting that she was in the room with him. "What I need is a good man or two on the job, to do some digging with me." He had these fragmentary thoughts between consultations with superintendents, talks with Divisional men, talks with Information, all the general routine of the CID. There was no outstanding case on the go at the moment, but there might be tonight or tomorrow; there would certainly be at least one sticky one this week—and a dozen times one of the Department's men was going to pray for more help, but wasn't likely to let Gideon play God, and so hear the prayer.

At half past six, when Riddell had been gone for an

hour, the telephone had been quiet for twenty minutes, and Gideon was looking through some reports and making notes and queries, the door opened and Rogerson came in. Gideon's first thought was that Rogerson looked very pale indeed, and that his eyes seemed too bright.

"Busy, George?"

"Just finishing."

"Didn't think you ever finished." Rogerson closed the door, went to Riddell's desk and leaned against it. He watched Gideon sign a couple of letters and fold them into their envelopes, then he went on: "You've cooked your goose, George. Why the dickens didn't you tell me you were going to come out with that bombshell?"

"Didn't know myself," answered Gideon, and concealed the way his heart dropped at that 'you've cooked your goose'. It sounded as if Rogerson had been talking to the Commissioner. "Needed saying, anyhow."

"Pity I didn't say it," Rogerson said; "but if I weighed in too much it would have looked like a put-up job. George, I was going to tell you today that I'm going to have to throw my hand in. I spent yesterday with two specialists, and they give me twelve months unless I drop everything and go to grass. I spent half an hour this morning telling the Old Man that he'd be crazy to look farther than you as my successor. God knows what he thinks now."

"Can't have a rebel AC," said Gideon, and made himself grin. "He wouldn't have had me anyhow."

"Why not?"

"Wrong tie."

"Don't be a fool," Rogerson said. "All the Old Man wants is results."

"We'll have a chance to see," said Gideon, and then realised that he had been so preoccupied with the way this would affect him he had hardly noticed that 'they gave me twelve months unless I drop everything and go to grass'. How self-centered could man be? "I hope you're not serious about those doctors," he finished belatedly.

"Believe it or not, I am. So is my wife, who's delivered an ultimatum; I'm to give up quickly."

"I'm not going to believe it," Gideon said. "I'm damned sorry, anyhow." He felt awkward, and the gleam of humour in Rogerson's eyes did nothing to help.

"It's time I was taken in hand," Rogerson said, and his smile was positively droll. "My heart isn't what it should be, but it's in the right place! What can I do to help you prepare this case for the Old Man?"

He meant: 'What can I do to get you out of this mess?' and also meant that he did not intend to dwell on his own troubles.

Gideon's grin seemed genuinely bright.

"Just get me a couple of secretaries and a few clerks to do the research," he answered.

"You'll do, George," Rogerson said, and went on soberly: "But you've probably misjudged Scott-Marle. You forgot he'd been trained in the Army. You don't kick against the pricks in the Army, and you don't argue with authority. Might have been better if you'd had a word with him in private first, but——"

"You're worrying too much about it," Gideon interrupted. "It needed saying, even though I might have chosen the time and place better. I'm going to have a hell of a job trying to convince him, but that's no reason why I shouldn't try. Think he'd like to get rid of me?"

"I'm damned sure he wouldn't, especially as I'm on the move," said Rogerson. "Well! I must be off. Thought I'd warn you. I'll be going at the end of the

31

month, so you've a week or two to show him how right you are. Shouldn't overdo it, though."

"I won't overdo it," Gideon assured him.

He knew exactly what Rogerson had meant: he had blotted his copybook badly, and must be very careful, or he would lose this chance of promotion. The AC took it for granted that at this stage Gideon wanted to step into his shoes. Gideon did not think much about that when, at seven o'clock, he finished the desk work and left the office after a word with the Chief Superintendent on duty for the night. He knew his own reactions very well, and knew that his subconscious pondering and reasoning often enabled him to see the solution to a case which had been puzzling the yard for a long time. He deliberately left a problem to 'soak,' knowing that he would do a great deal of subconscious thinking about it, and that the result would force its way into his conscious mind at the most unexpected time.

Had his manpower shortage been soaking? Had his outburst been the result of deep subconscious thought and anxiety?

Whether it was or not, he had to go and tell his wife, and prepare her for a dull evening companion. He was getting into his car, which was parked in the courtyard, when Joe Bell turned in at the iron gates. Gideon waited until Joe, looking rather tired, drew up alongside him.

"Going home already?"

"Just having an afternoon off," retorted Gideon, and Big Ben began to chime seven. "How's Eric Jones? All crocodile tears and promise of good behaviour if he gets just one more chance?"

"As a matter of fact, George, I've a nasty feeling that between the time he left here yesterday and the time we picked him up, he salted away about fifteen hundred quid," Bell said. "I don't know whether we'll be able to find that, either."

"Good God!" exclaimed Gideon.

"You don't exactly look depressed about it," Bell observed.

"You'd be surprised how depressed I am," said Gideon. "Anything else special?"

"Only one job," Bell reported. "I've arranged for Syd Taylor to work overtime, he's watching for Micky the Slob. Don't argue about signing his overtime chit when it comes in, will you?"

"I won't argue," Gideon promised, but he didn't smile. "Is Syd on his own?"

"Yes."

"Shouldn't there be two men after Micky?"

"Oh, I don't think it'll matter," said Bell. "Syd knows what he's about, and if he thinks there's the slightest danger, he'll send for help. Can't afford two men to watch where one will do, didn't you know?" Bell kept a straight face. "We nearly lost a certain Eric Jones because of that last night. Remember?"

"Go and check with the Night Super, and see if he can spare another man to join Syd Taylor," Gideon said. "If he can't, make sure that the Division checks with Taylor regularly, and ask Squad and Q cars in that district to keep an eye open. Micky the Slob can be a nasty customer."

"See what you mean," agreed Bell, "but Taylor can look after himself. I'll see what I can do, anyhow."

"Good," said Gideon.

For ten of his twenty-minute drive home he was thinking not of the overall problem but of Detective Sergeant Syd Taylor, one of the older sergeants on the Force. First and last, Gideon was a detective and a policeman, and his interest was in cases and criminals, in detectives and the job; administration came second.

He was uneasy about Taylor only because he would have been uneasy about any one man watching for a near-cretin like Micky the Slob.

Many men at the Yard and in the Division feared that one day Micky the Slob would do murder.

A switch of thoughts carried Gideon back to contemplation of the fact that he had to tell Kate exactly how he had stuck his neck out. He could not be sure whether she would say he ought to retract as soon as he could, and so safeguard his present position, or advise him to stick to his decision. Four hundred pounds a year, even with income tax and other deductions taken off, made a bid difference to comfort and a sense of security. Their large family—they had six children living and one had died—had made it impossible to save until a few years ago; now they were both saving and spending more, and living a pleasant life.

"She'll leave it to me," Gideon told himself, and then thought almost idly about Syd Taylor.

One thing troubled him more than anything else about the man; he must be tired. He would be able to cope if he were fresh, but could he tonight?

"The trouble is that I want something to go wrong," Gideon grumbled to himself. "Time I shook myself out of it."

He was nearing the turning in King's Road which led to his home, when he had to slow down behind a parked car, and this happened to be opposite the newspaper shop which served his home with the daily and evening newspapers. It was run by an old couple who were reliable with deliveries, but who did not worry much about changing the placards outside the window. One of these was three weeks old at least, and read:

CHILD KILLER STILL AT LARGE

34

That was the Bournsea job. A seven-year-old girl had been lured from her friends by a man whom no adult had seen; the child's body had been found, two days later, after a search which had stretched the nearby divisions and the Yard to danger-point. The child had been criminally assaulted and strangled; an ugly job. There was not a policeman in the country who would not work through night after night to find the beast who had committed the crime. Whether he was insane or not, they hated him with a kind of personal hatred.

The killer was still at large, so the old poster was not really dated.

Gideon had reviewed the investigation only two days ago, after the Yard Superintendent and his two aides, a Detective Inspector and a Detective Sergeant, had been recalled from Bournsea, where they had been assigned to help the local police. Although he had not thought of it at the time, Gideon knew that if the Yard had been able to call on plenty of reserve staff, he would not have withdrawn the trio; but after three weeks without result, it had seemed reasonable to leave the job to the local chaps, promising specific help if it were needed.

Gideon made a mental note of that, and then drove on and passed the newspaper shop and that poster.

CHILD KILLER STILL AT LARGE

The hell of it would be if another child was taken.

The killer still at large was sitting in a deckchair on Bournsea Beach. The sands were truly golden in the evening sun, the beach was comparatively empty, for it was nearly dinnertime in the resort's hotels and boarding-houses, and the restaurants and cafés were full. Most families had gone away by then, but some children played.

There was a group of four—three girls and a boy. The boy and two of the girls were nine or ten, and more adventurous than the youngest girl, who had shining, fair hair, red, round cheeks, and curiously rosebud-shaped lips. She wore just a pair of faded pink pants, and her little body was firm and beautifully brown.

The killer watched her at the water's edge.

The other children played fifty yards out in the sea, laughing and screaming, splashing and ducking each other. The smallest child turned, as all children will, when a dog went racing across the sands, and she crossed her arms over her unformed breasts and stood frightened, for the dog was nearly as tall as she.

The killer jumped up.

"It's all right," he called. "It's all right, don't worry." He shooed the dog, a happy-looking mongrel, part spaniel and part setter, and went to the little girl. "He won't hurt you," he assured her. "He's a very friendly chap."

Bright dark-blue eyes made it clear that the child doubted it.

"Look," said the killer, and took a bag of sweets out of his pocket. He put a toffee on one hand and held it out to the dog, who put its head on one side, showed its pink tongue and white teeth, made quite a job of getting the toffee off, and then began to chew as if he were used to toffee sticking to his teeth.

The child laughed.

"Like a toffee?" asked the man.

"Yes, *please*."

"Take one," he offered, and held out the bag. As she took one, he asked: "Do you often come and swim here?"

"My brother and sisters swim—I can't swim," she announced. "I can paddle."

"You'll be able to swim one day, too. Do you come every day?"

"Nearly every day," she answered.

"One of these days perhaps I'll teach you to swim," he promised, and his hand strayed to her lovely hair; he patted her head, and then left her, sitting down for another ten minutes before going off.

He whistled faintly, and the carefree mongrel, not much older than a puppy, followed him.

3

SYD TAYLOR

Syd Taylor knew that he was being watched, as well as watching; and it did not worry him at all. Thirty-one years in the service of the Metropolitan Police, twenty of them in the Criminal Investigation Department, had taught him nearly everything he needed to know about his and any other police job. He was fifty-three, big, as hard and muscular as most men fifteen years younger. Physical fitness was his religion. He knew all the holds of ju-jutsu; he had won the MP heavyweight boxing championship eight years in a row, and had never been defeated—even today, although he had not entered for twelve years, he was likely to get into any final he tried for. He had a black belt, being one of the earliest judo enthusiasts in England. He could walk, run, jump and fight with anyone, and his athletic prowess had made him a major figure at the Yard.

If rough stuff threatened, send for Syd Taylor.

He had a wife, four children and a son-in-law. He had often been heard to say that he did not want to rise a step higher in the cid; he was a first-class sergeant, but didn't like responsibility and seldom wielded it well. He was given as much respect as many superintendents, most chief inspectors and all detective inspectors, and in those thirty-one years he had never seriously broken rule or regulation; he was a work-to-the-book man and could quote regulations against any Yard lawyer.

Everyone in the Force liked Syd, but a great number of people outside it had good reason to dislike him, because he did not hesitate to use his strength if it was necessary. Once he had fought with Micky the Slob and two men almost as powerful, had broken Micky's nose and another man's ribs, and driven all three off. He was afraid of nothing with two fists.

He knew a great deal about Micky the Slob.

The nickname was justified, for Micky was a short man with powerful shoulders, very powerful arms, a short neck and a big, flabby face. He had the look almost of a cretin, with porcine eyes, very fair lashes, hardly any eyebrows. He was not a cretin, but very cunning although not at all original. He lived in NE Division, near the docks, and his speciality was organising smuggling and pilfering from ships. He recruited his men from foreign crews, foreign sailors waiting for a ship, lascars and some of the more dissatisfied dock workers. He preferred to work with gangs, which made it more difficult for the police to separate him from the rest. He would arrange for twenty or thirty men working on a ship, either from the crew or from the docks, to gang up on anyone who wanted to search him or the particular ship, and make it impossible.

He had been inside twice, once for three and once for five years. If he were caught again, he would go down for ten years, and possibly longer. He never hesitated to use violence if cornered, but did not like fighting for its own sake.

Ten days ago, he had fought a running battle with the Dock Police, injuring two of them, and had escaped with a small packet of industrial diamonds from Holland; he had probably got away with a dozen packets during the past five years, but this time he had been caught red-handed. The police knew the places where he was likely to be hiding out and suspected one in particular—a big, rambling old house near the docks, now mainly one-room flatlets, with one or two larger flats. The police had searched this house twice, without finding Micky, but there was a strong possibility that he had managed to hide. So it had become a war of attrition, and the house was kept under surveillance by day and night. It was on a corner, and at the back was a high warehouse wall. There was only one way in which Micky could possibly escape, so it was sufficient to watch the house from one position, on an opposite corner.

On this corner was a dockside café.

Syd Taylor sometimes sat in a window-seat; sometimes strolled up and down; at other times, relieved by a Divisional man, he went off for an hour. It was simply a matter of patience; knowing Micky the Slob well, Taylor was quite sure that his own patience would outlast the other's.

Sooner or later Micky would break out, he might even try to get aboard a ship and out of the country, but that was not likely. He lived apart from his wife, but she was being watched, too, which meant that the job took the combined efforts of two men most of the time, and three during the relief periods.

Taylor knew the district inside out. He had spent years at the Divisional Station when on the beat, knew half of the men who patronised the café by name, and most of them by sight. Nine out of ten were as honest as he; he felt absolutely safe while he was there by day, and believed that if trouble was coming, it would be at dusk when day was nearly done. Some of Slob's men would try to distract his attention before he could summon help, and the Slob would slip away into London's darkness. It might be weeks or months before he was traced again.

Taylor also knew that before long the Yard would have to take off the watch; Micky the Slob wasn't that important, and if a big job blew up, he would get a chance to disappear.

That evening, about the time that Gideon was talking to Bell at the Yard, Taylor came out of the café, and a big docker approached from along the street.

"Hullo, Syd, still wearing out the soles of your feet?"

"Giving them a bit of exercise," agreed Taylor.

"Pity you ain't got something better to do."

"Nothing better than putting a man behind bars," Taylor quipped.

The docker grinned and pushed past him, then whispered out of the side of his mouth: "Be careful around ten tonight, Syd." No one could see that his lips moved and no one else could hear the words.

Taylor grunted, and strolled along the street, more than ever certain of the fact that he was being watched from that house on the corner. The next patrol car and the next copper who passed could take or send a message to Division or the Yard; instead of being on edge, Taylor felt an anticipatory glow of excitement.

If this was going to be the night, he'd be ready; and he could thank his friends among the dockers.

Across the road, in an attic-room where he could not be seen from the street unless he stood right in front of the tiny window, Slob grinned as he saw the docker push past Taylor. He had a big, loose, slobbery mouth; that was why his nickname was so apt. Even his little eyes smiled, and he turned to a man who had just come into the room.

"Bert just told him."

"That's the boy."

"Get everything ready," Slob said. He slurred his words but they were clear enough and he turned away from the window.

Taylor was never left completely alone for more than twenty minutes; someone was always passing. A Squad car, back from a false alarm at a furrier's warehouse in the Mile End Road, made a detour and slowed down by the café. That was at twenty-five minutes past seven. Taylor, reading a newspaper as he leaned against the wall near the café, moved to the car. He was careful not to speak until he was bending down, and no one could lip-read what he said; the most unlikely people had remarkable talent.

"Having a nice quiet time?" asked the Flying Squad driver.

"Until ten o'clock."

"What's that?"

"I've had a squeak," Taylor told him, and added with obvious pride: "That's what comes of having friends. You want to try it some time. See that I've got company from about nine-fifteen onwards, will you? I'd say that's the most likely time that Slob'll try for a break."

"When it's murky," the driver remarked. "Okay, Syd. I'll give the Yard a flash, and check everything when I get back there. Any idea whether it's going to be big or small?"

"Assume it'll be a big crowd."

"Attaboy!"

Taylor went back to the wall and the newspaper as

42

the car drove off. He experienced a tingling of even greater excitement, and felt not only satisfied but in a mood to congratulate himself for wearing down Micky the Slob before the Yard gave it up as a bad job. He did his regulation twenty deep breaths every half hour, and kept flexing his muscles, already spoiling for a fight; for he was quite sure in his own mind that there would be one.

The next man likely to come round was the sergeant from the Division, calling on the men on the beat; he was due about eight o'clock.

A girl came out of one of the houses near the corner, and walked briskly towards him. She was very short and rather plump, with an enormous bosom sheathed in a thin, thigh-clinging white jumper. She had big, curving hips, very small feet and startling trim ankles, and her colouring was remarkably vivid. Taylor had seen her dozens of times before, and usually she bobbed past him, with a smile or a quip. As always Taylor raised his hat, with exaggerated politeness. She gave him a wide smile, and as she drew up, asked the familiar question:

"Aren't you tired of holding that wall up?"

Taylor was ready for that.

"If it means seeing you twice a day, sweetheart, I'll hold it up for the rest of the year."

She stopped, and smiled up at him; she had a pert little face and shiny, smiling black eyes.

"Proper Don Jewan, that's what you're getting," she retorted. "It's a pity you have to waste your time, I wouldn't mind treating you to the palais."

"We'll go dancing some other time."

"Don't exert yourself," she said. "Seriously, Syd, why don't you give this lark up? The Slob's not over there, he ducked long ago. You're making a mistake,

43

honest you are. I didn't think you chaps at the Yard had so much time to waste."

"Now go on and remind me that it's really the tax-payer's money we're spending, such as yours," said Taylor. A motor cycle was coming along the street, scorching, with a rider and a pillion passenger; he glanced at it, but did not recognise either of the youths on it; they were not in the Slob's circle as far as he knew. He looked back at the girl. "How much did he drop you to try and make me take a walk?"

"I'm not on his side, I'm just an innocent by-stander," she declared promptly. "I just don't like to think of you wasting your time. He went a couple of days ago, when one of those stooges of yours was on duty."

Taylor wondered, a little uneasily, whether she knew what she was talking about. Then he remembered the docker's message, and decided that she was trying to put him off his guard. She might have succeeded but for the tip he'd just had.

"Care to make a statement?" he asked.

The motor cycle was almost level with him and the girl, now, but Taylor suspected nothing until, quite suddenly, she opened her painted mouth wide, and screamed. Taylor was taken completely unawares. She screamed again and then raised her plump, clenched fists and beat him about the face. He grabbed her wrists, to fend her off. He was just aware of the motor cycle stopping, and saw the two youths jump off, but the girl was giving him too much to think about; now she was clawing at his cheeks, and scratching him badly, and she was still screaming.

It was the oldest trick in the repertoire. Taylor felt desperate, knowing exactly what was coming next and was almost powerless to prevent it. If he could only get the girl off him, he would have a chance. It was amazing how difficult it was to be really rough with a woman, but he gripped her wrists at last, twisted, and sent her staggering back against the café window. He swung round towards the two youths, but they were very close, and one had a spanner raised head high.

There was only one hope—attack.

Taylor leapt at the man with the spanner, but as he did so, a man he did not see slipped out of the café and hooked his legs from under him. He fell heavily, and a boot smacked into his cheek.

He heard a car coming up.

Through a blur of tears of pain and blood from a cut over his eye he saw the car stop by the corner, knew exactly what was going to happen, made a tremendous effort to get to his feet, but was dragged down. As he fell, he felt those boots again; then an agonising pain stabbed through his head, and he knew that all the hatred that the Slob's men had stored up for him was pouring out.

He tried to cover up.

Not a sound escaped his lips.

It was all over in two minutes.

Micky the Slob was moving off in the car, the motorcyclists were on their way, the six or seven other men who had come from round the corner were dispersing, the girl had disappeared.

Taylor lay in a crumpled heap, very still, and the first to approach him was the woman who ran the café; she sent one of her children to fetch the police.

4

GIDEON'S KATE

Gideon wondered which of his children still living at home would be in, and how long it would be before he could have half an hour alone with Kate. These light evenings, there was a good chance that she would be alone. She would certainly be in, and ready for him; she had a genius for always looking bright and fresh when he arrived, whether it was five o'clock on a rare early home-coming, or ten or eleven, which happened once or twice most weeks. He did not expect to be called out tonight, but parked his car outside the terraced house in Hurlingham, near the Thames, which he had moved into when he and Kate had first married.

It looked attractive, for the red brick had been pointed last autumn, and this spring the painters had made quite a job of the woodwork; black and white, on Kate's request. The windows shone, as if Kate had cleaned them herself. The tiled porch, made of large mosaic, had a polished look, too. It was an old but comfortable house, and now had everything he wanted.

He slid his key into the lock, and stepped inside; there was a faint sound of radio music—unless it was the television. He hung his hat on the hallstand, where the children's clothes should be; only one or two school hats hung there, so the indications were that they were all out. The living-room was at the back of the house, approached by the passage which ran alongside the staircase, and the door was ajar. He opened it quietly. Kate was sitting in an easy chair, some men's socks on her lap, a needlework basket by her side, watching the seventeen-inch television; a coloured soprano began to sing, clear, pure notes.

"Not bad, is she?" asked Gideon.

Kate started, and turned her head. "Oh, you fool, you made me jump."

"Sorry, dear." He went forward and kissed her on the forehead. He hoped that there wasn't a programme which she was intent on seeing, he did not want to turn off the set deliberately, and would much rather be casual about what he had to do. "Don't get up, there's no hurry for five minutes."

"I'll just see this," Kate said. "It'll be over by half past. Had a good day?"

Gideon didn't answer.

Kate looked at him sharply, but he was watching the singer, while squatting on the edge of the big table. The room was large and narrow, and there was an assortment of easy chairs, one for every member of the family. Leading off it was the kitchen, where the family had breakfast and supper, often only one or two eating at a time.

When Kate turned back to the screen, Gideon studied her. She looked fine, with her good, healthy colouring, and a rather dominating nose. Her black hair was turning grey at the sides, and was very thick; it was a little greasy now. Her hands, still for once, although the needle was between her fingers, were long and not really rough with housework. There had been a time when she had not been able to afford much help

47

even in the mornings, but now they had a regular daily, and their two elder daughters did a share of the evening chores.

The coloured singer stopped, curtsied, smiled. Kate leaned forward, switched off the set, and said:

"What did you have for lunch?"

"Couple of sandwiches."

"I thought as much," Kate said. "It's time you realised that you ought to have a good meal at midday, George, you're too old to manage on sandwiches. I've a steak that won't take long, though. Come and help me cook it."

Just right.

"Be with you in a minute," Gideon said.

He went upstairs, washed, ran a comb through his own iron-grey hair, and looked at himself in the mirror. No one could deny that his was a strong face. He fingered his jowl, which was thickening, and gave a wry kind of grin. "Now for it," he said aloud, and went briskly down the stairs. When he reached the kitchen the steak was beginning to spit under the grill, and fat was bubbling in a saucepan, a basket of uncooked chips was waiting to go in. "Looks good," said Gideon. "All the others had supper?"

"Yes."

"I'll lay it here, then." There was a small table with red formica top, and Gideon put out knives, forks and plates, fetched the bread and the butter, and finished as Kate dumped the chips into the boiling fat; there was a great hissing and a cloud of smoke. She backed away, then took the steak out, and basted it.

"I can open a tin of peas," she said.

"Never mind the peas," Gideon pulled out a kitchen chair which looked hardly big enough for him, and sat down, leaning one elbow against the table. "Feel like a confessional?"

48

"Now what have you been up to?" Kate looked at him intently, and he realised that she had sensed his mood almost as soon as he had come in.

He spoke very quietly.

"I'm not quite sure what the consequences will be, but I may get a kick in the pants. Downwards," he added, and then told her quietly, and his matter-of-fact manner gave the story an added vividness. Kate watched him most of the time, twice took the steak from the grill and turned it, without interrupting, and he was not quite sure of the story's effect on her when he finished: "It's funny in a way. The only hope I've got of proving my argument is to work like the devil to prepare it, and I've hardly time to turn round as it is."

Kate said: "If they could be such fools as to accept your resignation, you'd be better off at a Division, George. But they won't."

"Wish I could be so sure."

"Well, I'm sure, and in any case, someone had to say it," Kate declared, and suddenly he was at ease again. She stabbed a chip with a fork, nipped it between her fingers, shook her hand and went on: "They need another two or three minutes. I don't know how many of the others work like you do, but you do twice as much as you should, and if you go on much longer you'll really overdo it. You've only got to get blood pressure, or get that backache trouble again, and you'll have to slacken off." She flashed a smile at him, and the smile did as much as her words to bring a mood of deep satisfaction; he should have been more sure of her. "You want to let *me* go and talk to the Commissioner, or better still, start a campaign among the neglected wives. How's that for an idea?"

They laughed.

"I'm half serious," Kate said, as she drained the fat off the chips into a big saucepan. "Take the steak out, and cut a piece off for me. I don't want too much, I had a good lunch."

"You mean you're afraid of getting fat?"

She looked at his waistline.

"Well, you aren't, you're two inches too much round there already." Between them they dished up and sat down, before Kate went on: "I shouldn't even begin to worry, George, especially with Rogerson going. They can't risk losing the Assistant Commissioner and the Commander at the same time. Did you want the AC's job?"

"Want me to want it? It's worth another thousand a year."

"No, I don't," Kate answered, flatly. "I think it would be a mistake. Even now you grumble because you've so much administration to do, and can't give enough thought to the investigation side. If you took that job over it would be mostly administration. I'm not sure you'd get along too well with the other ACs either. They'd be nice enough, but you would probably feel like a fish out of water, and hate it because of the social differences. You may not realise it, George, but beneath that horny old hide of yours you're as sensitive as Prudence." Prudence was their eldest daughter. "Now, eat it while it's hot."

Gideon thought: 'Well, I couldn't have hoped for anything better.' Kate was making quite sure that he felt like that, of course; and probably they wouldn't be so silent after all; she might have some suggestions which would be worth following up.

The steak was just right; not too tender, just the thing to get his teeth into.

They had started to clear away when the telephone bell rang. One instrument was in the living-room, another in the hall, a third extension was in Gideon's bedroom. Gideon went into the living-room. This might

50

be for one of the children, but there was always the possibility that it would be from the Yard; and if it were, it would mean an emergency.

"Gideon . . ."

"What?" he cried, and it was not often he raised his voice.

"All right," he said a minute later. "I'll come at once." He rang off, but did not move away from the telephone. Instead, he stared at the open door leading to the kitchen, and Kate appeared, as if he had willed her to. He dialled another number, as she drew nearer, obviously affected by the look on his face. "I'm calling Rogerson," he said. "Syd Taylor was beaten up about ten minutes ago, it looks as if he might not come round. I want to make sure that they get the best surgeon they can."

Kate said, "*Syd*," in a tone which told Gideon that she was thinking not only of Syd and his reputation, but also of his wife and his family.

The telephone was ringing: *brrr-brrr; brrr-brrr*.

He hoped Rogerson wouldn't be out.

"Why don't you let me tell him, and you hurry on," Kate suggested.

"Good idea," said Gideon. "Thanks, dear, I'll get back as soon as I can, but I may be pretty late. I shouldn't wait up." He handed her the telephone, gave her a little squeeze, and went off.

Kate saw him take his hat off the peg in the hall, and saw him open the front door and go out. She knew that he had almost forgotten her, and knew how deeply he would feel about this crime.

She said aloud: "At least he had a good meal."

* * *

Gideon knew the Yard by night almost as well as he knew it by day. There were fewer people about, most of the civil staff being home, but there was a greater sense of urgency and expectancy. Two Squad cars were waiting in the courtyard, ready to race off, some plain-clothes men were walking across to Cannon Row, with a handcuffed man between them. Gideon recognised an old lag, Larry Day, who must have done a job that evening and been picked up at once. It was still broad daylight, and most of the crimes were only in the minds of the men who were going to commit them; Gideon knew that almost every form of crime and vice was going to take place during the next twelve hours. It always did. That was the reason for his forthrightness and for his anxiety; this constant, bitter war. Unless you were in it day after day and sometimes hour by hour, you did not realise how ceaseless it was, how dangerous and how deadly.

Deadly?

Whether Syd Taylor lived or died, whether murder was committed anywhere in London tonight, did not really matter. Murder was the crime that caught the attention and won the newspaper space; that and the big holdups, the sensational robberies; but they were only a fractional part of the war. If he wanted to be pompous he would say that crime was gnawing continually at the walls of society, and kept breaching those walls. It was impossible to estimate the number of criminals in London, but safe to say that they had doubled in fifteen years; far too many people committed first, second and even third crimes without being caught, and so emboldened themselves and others.

There were a few 'big' criminals, but they were not the main problem. Few really clever men turned to crime deliberately, although some drifted into it, usually to try to recoup business losses. Half-clever criminals could do a lot of harm before they were caught, particularly those who were unknown to the police when they began to work, but the bitter war of attrition was with the little crook, who earned his livelihood from crime.

Out among London's two million homes and eight million people, hundreds of families were about to be robbed of money which few could afford. Listening to the radio or watching the television, the war would be brought into their home by crafty, cunning, stealthy men. The fact that if interrupted a thief might use violence was a consequence of the problem, not the problem itself. The fact that people were not safe from burglary in their homes was the heart of the matter.

Among the crowds in the West End, the dips would soon be busy, and the pros would be out in swarms. Fools of men, eager for a woman, would submit themselves to blandishments, drink too much, and be robbed of everything they had in their pockets.

There were so many facets to the war.

In a dozen places, behind a façade of respectability, the gaming was going on. Here and there a bank was being entered, and a big haul planned, but the infantry of crime remained the little men, the little women, many unsuspected and unknown.

Gideon went upstairs, passed his own office, and opened the door of one just round the corner. Here lights were blazing, the Night Superintendent in charge, Fred Champion, was at his desk, three men in their shirtsleeves were with him, two talking into telephones. It was a familiar kind of bedlam, but Champion greeted Gideon with a smile which seemed quite free from urgency or anxiety. He was thin and dark-haired, and rather saturnine-looking unless he was smiling. Like Riddell, he always dressed well, and usually wore brown; unlike Riddell, he had a quick mind.

"How is Syd?" Gideon asked.

"No fresh news, George."

"Where is he?"

"The Middlesex."

"Got anyone yet?"

"Not a hope."

That was the answer which Gideon had feared, the answer which made him want to say: 'We've got to get the Slob if we forget every other case we're on,' but that kind of emotional outburst wouldn't help. It reminded him that he was very edgy, and finding it difficult to take things as dispassionately as he should; that in itself made him a little uneasy, too.

"What's the report say?" He went round to Champion's side, and stood by the desk, towering over it.

"Bit sketchy, so far," Champion answered. "Apparently there was some trouble between Taylor and a girl. Two of the people in the café say he interfered with her as she walked past. We know that's a lie, but it tells us how they're going to play it: that Syd tried to play around with a girl, and two of her boy friends set about him. We can't get anything else yet. The woman who found him said she didn't notice anything. When our chaps got to the spot, there were only two people in the café near by, and they said they saw these two fellows on a motor-cycle. Judging from what we hear, a dozen men must have ganged up on Syd, but I doubt if we'll ever prove it."

"Sure the Slob left the house?"

"Two independent witnesses from the other end of the street say they saw a car drive off. Anyhow, we can take it for granted that it was laid on to get him away."

"Suppose so," grunted Gideon. "Who's at NE tonight?"

"Pratt."

"Call him, and tell him not to be surprised if he sees me about, will you?"

"Right, George." Champion knew that it would be a waste of time trying to persuade Gideon that he should not go over to the Division and the scene of the crime. Like most men who had come up from the ranks, at heart Gideon was still out on the job. Given any reasonable excuse he would go and see the spot, talk to suspects and witnesses, and in an almost miraculous way get to know the case and the circumstances better than anyone else.

"Tell Information to call me if there's any news of Syd," he said as he turned to go.

"I will."

"Anyone told his wife yet?"

"Thought we'd hold off until we knew what the odds were."

"Yes," Gideon agreed. "Who'll go?"

"Don't know."

"I will," Gideon said. He still stood in the doorway. "Much else on yet?"

"They picked up Larry Day. He heaved a brick through a jeweller's window in Bond Street."

"Fred," Gideon said abruptly, "we've got a problem, because we can't cover the ground. If you've time, check how many jobs we're handling with a man short, and then check with four or five divisions to find out how many men they're short—CID and the uniformed branch separately."

"What's this, a Gallup poll?" Champion demanded.

"Could be."

"Only way you'll ever get the extra staff you're after is by getting public opinion behind us," Champion declared, "and as we're not allowed to go after public opinion, there isn't a chance. It's no use applying common-or-garden logic. This is politics, my boy, and the politicians are screaming for economies. This time they're going to get it."

"Who's been talking to you?" asked Gideon.

"Just a little bird," Champion answered.

If he knew, then the fact that Gideon had let off steam at the conference that morning was all over the Yard. He should have realised that was likely. As far as he could tell, it made no difference—except that Champion had made him very thoughtful about public opinion. That was a point. First get something to rouse public opinion, and then cash in on it. But how?

Gideon went down to his car, and as he heaved his great body in, realised that there was a kind of excitement in his mind, a knowledge that what had happened to Taylor might be the turning-point in the fight he had on his hands. If Taylor died, it would be in every head-line tomorrow morning.

"What the devil's got into me?" Gideon asked himself savagely. "He mustn't die."

Syd Taylor's wife was a small, wiry, alert-looking woman, whom Gideon had met at the police ball, and occasionally at the police sports club. Obviously she knew as soon as she set eyes on him that he brought bad news. When he told her, he thought she would collapse; but she collected herself, and was soon ready to go to the hospital.

Even though he couldn't see Syd, she could wait; and two Yard men were there already.

The Divisional men were outside the East End café when Gideon drove up, soon after he had left the hospital. There was a diagram on the pavement, where Taylor had been found, and the whole area around the shop had been cordoned off. The woman café owner was complaining that no customers were able to get in, and she was going to claim compensation. A few dozen people stood about, including several children. The front door of the house where Micky the Slob had been staying was wide open, and Gideon saw the grinning man who lived there with his family. This was a sharp slap in the face for the police, and most of the bystanders were gloating.

Pratt, one of the NE Division's senior Chief Inspectors, was supervising the work. Three photographers were busy, and another man was taking plaster casts of footprints in the dirt at the side of the road. Several bloodstains, just brown smears, led from a patch of Taylor's coagulated blood.

Pratt was a big man with a good reputation, and the quality of perseverance rather than brilliance. He wore hornrimmed glasses, his black hair was heavily oiled and smeared down, and it would be easy to mistake him for a bookmaker's clerk.

He hurried across to Gideon.

"Was told you might look round, Mr. Gideon, very glad you've come. Any news of Taylor?"

"They're operating. They've one of the best surgeons, anyhow."

"I suppose that's something," Pratt said. He took off his glasses, which were badly smeared, and began to clean them with a spotless and beautifully laundered handkerchief. "The devil of it is I feel largely responsible. There was an official request for a man to stand in with Taylor, but I decided that it would probably be a waste of time, so I refused. No doubt that the Slob took a chance because there was only one man watching him."

"Couldn't agree more," said Gideon.

"Thing that worries me is, where's it going to end?"

asked Pratt. "I expect it worries you, too. It's about time the recruiting campaign really woke up; what's the use of plastering a few posters round the place, saying what a lovely life it is to be a policeman? Just tells people like Micky the Slob that we're hard up for men. Micky's not one of the brightest, but even he can see that. Some of the brighter boys are going to tell themselves that this is just their opportunity, that's my considered opinion." He talked rather like Worth wrote his reports. "A lot of people knew that Taylor was on his own, but most of them thought that he had someone else watching, out of sight. Now that it's so obvious that we could only spare one man to keep a lookout for Micky—well, I'd expect a lot of trouble in the next few weeks. Wouldn't you?"

"It wouldn't surprise me," Gideon agreed. "Any idea who would be most likely to take advantage of the situation?"

"Could name a dozen," Pratt answered.

If he could name a dozen criminals quick enough on the uptake to see and to seize any special opportunity, then the other East End and Central London Divisions could name at least three or four dozen between them. Deep down, Gideon knew, this had been responsible for the depth of his own feeling and for his outburst that morning. Once the well-trained, well-equipped army of criminals realised that the police could be caught on one foot, they would jump into the attack. It would not be organised because organised crime in London was very limited; but it would be spontaneous, and perhaps more dangerous.

"Name that dozen in a report, will you?" Gideon said, and switched the subject. "Any news of the girl?"

"She's been in digs at a house along the road, 57 Dock Street," Pratt answered. "Been there about three weeks. We've been after Micky the Slob for a

58

month, so it looks as if she was planted there. I can't get a really good description but I'll dig something out. If Taylor could make a statement, it might hold a lot. Think he's likely to come round?"

"Wish I knew," said Gideon.

He shook hands with Pratt, had a word with all the men working on the job, and went back to his car. Among the crowd, some of the people jeered, and there was a chorus of *Gee-up, Gee-Gee*. A wag cried: "Also ran, Gee-Gee!" and won his laugh from the crowd. At his car, Gideon turned, looked at them, and then startled them by grinning and waving. Puzzled people watched him as he drove off.

"Looks almost pleased with himself," a man said to Pratt.

"Just putting up a show." Pratt said.

But in fact, in a queer way, Gideon felt exhilarated; he was seeing a lot of things very clearly.

There were two sides even in this war.

He got away from the docks, pulled into the side of the road, and flicked on his radio. Information Room answered almost at once.

"Gideon," he announced. "Any news of Taylor?"

"None, sir."

"The Slob?"

"No, sir."

"Flash me if there is. Meanwhile, send a message to all Central London Divisions and to E1 and D1, say that I'll be calling. I'll do OP next, the E1, then work my way south of the river to CD, then north of the river. Got all that?"

"Yes, sir."

"Thanks," said Gideon, and flicked off, started the engine again, and got off to a quick start.

Suddenly, he was in a hurry.

* * *

That evening, the chid who played at the edge of the
sea on Bournsea Beach, while the older children swam
and dived and played, saw the big dog which liked toffees leaping across the sands toward her. This time, she
did not look so frightened, but was a little uncertain,
and glanced at the dog's owner, who was strolling down
from the promenade. He reached the child, took out
the bag of sweets, and said:

"Would you like to give him a toffee tonight?"

She looked even more uncertain.

"Try," he urged. "He won't bit you, I promise.
Look, I'll hold your hand."

"All right," the child agreed.

The man unwrapped a toffee, put it on the palm of
her small hand, then placed his hand beneath it, and
held hers firmly. He placed his free hand, very gently,
against the child's round little belly and, standing behind her, pressed her against him.

She stood stiff with fear of the dog.

It put its head on one side, took the toffee, and began
to chew.

"See, it's easy," the man said.

The seven-year-old suddenly laughed with delight,
looked into his eyes and said:

"I gave it to him! He took it away from me!"

"I told you he would, didn't I?"

"Yes, you told me," she agreed, and there was the
birth of great trust in her bright eyes. "You said he
would, and he did." She was young even for her age,
and had a true simplicity. "Can *I* have a toffee?"

"Yes. Like two?"

"Yes, please."

"Here you are," the man said, and patted her head,
patted her bottom, and then went back to his chair and

sat, back to the promenade, watching her. Very few people were about, and the beach attendants were all having their time off; most of them were finished for the day.

When the elder children came back, dripping sea-water pearls, the man and the dog had gone. The seven-year-old did not tell them about the toffees she had had, but boasted gleefully about the dog she had fed out of her own hand.

"Garn," said the elder sister, "you're only making it up. Come on, we'd better hurry, or Ma'll give it to us." They towelled themselves vigorously and then made their way off the beach towards the back streets of Bournsea, where they lived. Their mother, who went out to work from eight until half past six, would expect supper ready when she arrived home.

Their father, a merchant sailor, was at sea.

It was not really surprising that on his jaunt that night, Gideon saw another of the placards which had caught his attention at his own newspaper shop.

CHILD KILLER STILL AT LARGE

He hardly gave it a thought, for he had so much to do.

Keith Ryman was in a night club near his home when he saw Rab Stone, who came towards him, grinning broadly. There was a bubble of conversation, and no one appeared to take any particular interest in the two men.

"Well, how're tactics?" demanded Stone. "Coming along okay?"

"Just about to bear fruit," Ryman answered. "What's making you so happy!"

"I've seen Charlie Daw," answered Stone, "and it's all over the town, the cops are pulling their punches because they're short-staffed. And it'll get worse before it gets better."

"That wouldn't surprise me," Ryman said. "We'll make our packet and be out of the business long before there's anything to worry about."

"Any specific ideas yet?" Stone inquired.

"When I'm ready, I'll tell you," Ryman said.

5

FIRST BLOW

Hopkinson, of NE Division, was contemporary with Gideon; they had joined the Force in the same week, and followed almost identical careers to the Yard, until Hopkinson had been given a Divisional Superintendency; there was not a better man in charge of any London Division. He was short, barely five feet nine, rather small-boned, and bald as a coot. His movements were brisk and sometimes he gave the impression that he was nervous; but he did not know the meaning of nerves. He had a widespread Division, and only that part of it which was close to OP across the river and had common boundary with QR, was really densely populated; there he found most of his trouble, most of his bad men.

He pumped Gideon's hand.

"Feel like a nip, George, or rather have a cuppa?"

"A nip'll suit me fine," said Gideon, and dropped into a big armchair; this was one of the few divisions where they had a chair large enough for him to sit in comfort. "Thanks," he said a minute later, and lifted his glass. "Here's to a busy night."

They drank.

"Always on the go," declared Hopkinson.

"You don't know what it is to be busy," Gideon scoffed. "Hoppy, I know you think Pratt's a pain in the neck, but he jolted me just now. Said that once it was known we really had only one man watching Micky the Slob, a lot of the boys would try to cash in, so we could expect a big bulge in the graph."

"S'right enough. How long have you been letting other people do your thinking for you?"

"He reckons that he could name a dozen boys in his manor who would be quick enough on the uptake to get moving right away."

"So could I."

"Thanks," said Gideon. "Go through the ones in your manor, pick out the bright boys who might see the chance, and pull 'em in, even if it's only for questioning. See if you can find a handy little charge to put 'em on remand for the usual eight days. Put as many of them as you can out of the way, and scare the others into behaving themselves for a few days. Got the idea?"

Hopkinson had bright little blue eyes.

"Pratt didn't think that up," he commented. "I'll see what I can do, George."

"You just do it," Gideon said. "And if you can pick any of them up tonight, fix that too."

"I'll bring a few in, I've got a few charges up my sleeve," Hopkinson told him. "I hoped that I'd get something bigger against most of the slobs, but I can see your point. If we can get our blow in first, it'll discourage them."

"Right," Gideon said.

He went off, feeling much better humoured than he had expected to.

That night he covered eight Divisions as well as made a visit to the City Police, where the Superintendent in charge was as willing to co-operate as any of the Metropolitan Police chiefs. It was half past eleven before he finished, after being on the go all the time, talking to each man with the same enthusiasm. Some superintendents off duty for the night had even come in when they heard he was going to call.

He had the whole of London to cross when he left NE Division, and yawned a dozen times as he sent the car along the Embankment, touching fifty most of the time. It was a beautiful night, there wasn't a cloud anywhere, and a crescent moon was shining on the river. This was London as he loved it, the London that seemed to belong to him. He slowed down, but did not stop to get out. He felt very tired, and realised that high pressure at the end of the day took much more out of him than it had a year or so back. But at least he could feel sure that he had launched that attack, and won a few days of grace.

In a way, a sudden eruption of crime would have strengthened his battle with the Commissioner, but although he knew that, Gideon did not think seriously about it. Tactically, he'd won this round; strategically, he still had a big fight on his hands; but he was feeling in the right mood for a tussle.

Although it was midnight when he reached home, a light was on in the living-room. Malcolm, his teenage son, was curled up in an armchair with a book, and continental music was coming over the radio. Malcolm put the book down, but didn't get up.

"Hallo, Dad."

"Where's your mother?"

"Gone to bed, she said I could finish this chapter."

"She didn't mean the book." Gideon said. "Put a kettle on and I'll make a cup of tea. Like one?"

"No, thanks," said Malcolm, "but why don't you go up? I'll bring the tea. Mum won't be asleep yet."

"Thanks, good idea," said Gideon, and went upstairs.

There was no news of Taylor and no interruption during the night, or up to nine o'clock in the morning, when Gideon left for the office; and no special news when he arrived.

Riddell was there, spruce, but obviously on his guard. 'Oh, lor',' thought Gideon as he said good morning and rounded his desk. There were twice as many reports on it as usual—two big piles. He knew what they were, but badly missed the summary of the reports which his normal assistants would have had ready. But he was in no mood to start putting Riddell in his place."

"I simply haven't the time to go through all of them," Riddell confessed. "I know how you like it done, but——"

"Forget it."

"The Central Divisions appear to have gone mad," Riddell said. "They're pulling in suspects by the dozen."

It was impossible to explain to him. Gideon tried new tactics, grinned, told him to pull up a chair, and said they would go through the memos together. Riddell sat down, and picked up a pencil; Gideon saw that he had already drawn up a kind of report form, different from any that Gideon had seen before.

"I thought you would like an analysis of arrests made as there were so many." Riddell was cautious.

"Good idea," said Gideon. "Shall I sing 'em out? Here's ST Division, eleven arrests, all minor charges, let's see—six indictable, the rest non-indictable. Got those headings?"

"Yes."

Perhaps he was a good Records man, square peg in the round hole.

"Right," Gideon said. "Now——"

Telephones started to ring, and they were interrupted a dozen times, but within an hour Gideon could see the whole picture. He sent for the Superintendents and the Chief Inspectors who had been out on normal work, heard each one out, made suggestions about cases, picked up odd items of information and stored these away in his memory. That was his greatest asset; a memory which not only stored but pigeon-holed. There were no new major crimes in the reports, and continuing inquiries ranged from murder to bank robberies, from a solicitor's fraud to West End vice. When he had talked to every man with a report to make, he put in a call to the hospital.

"Just heard a report to the secretary about that," the operator told him.

Gideon tensed.

'Good or bad?"

"Had as good a night as could be expected, but he's in a very serious condition."

"Ah," Gideon grunted. "Could be worse. Mr. Rogerson in?"

"No, sir, he expects to be in about noon."

"Thanks," said Gideon.

He took five minutes' respite, then studied the summary which he and Riddell had made. Riddell was now sitting at his own small desk, taking down a telephone message. The office was very quiet. Gideon saw that Riddell had totalled everything up; twenty-seven arrests had been made as a result of the new tactics, nineteen of them on non-indictable charges, and thirty-one men and three women had been at the different Divisional Headquarters for questioning.

Riddell put the receiver down.

"That was a report from Ollson up at Manchester. There has been no major charge, he thinks that he might be able to come down tomorrow and go into it with you, if you think it would be wise."

"Tell him to stay put until I send for him," Gideon said. "That'll please him."

"I'll send him a teletype message," promised Riddell. "There's one other message. The PRO says he'd like to have a talk to you. Are you free for lunch?"

"His treat?"

"He said, 'Ask Mr. Gideon if he would like to lunch with me'. If so, will you meet him in the main hall at twelve forty-five."

"Thanks," said Gideon. "Tell him yes."

That was at half past eleven. He had no idea what the Press Relations Officer wanted. The man was on the Civil Staff, and most of the CID's public relations was handled by the Inspector in the Back Room; this Inspector would soon be clamouring for a statement to give to the pressmen who waited on the Embankment, thirsting for news.

Now that the rush of the morning's work was over, Gideon had a reaction which he didn't much like; a kind of mental vacuum. He was really on tenterhooks for a call from the Commissioner, and it didn't come; he expected one from Rogerson, too, and Rogerson didn't call.

He put a call through to Rogerson's office.

"I'm sorry, sir," said his secretary, "but he has been with the Commissioner for the last half-hour and I believe they are lunching together."

"All right, thanks," said Gideon. "I'll call him again this afternoon."

It was not often that he felt any sense of anxiety, but he found it difficult to settle, and would have given a lot to know what his two superiors were saying. In a way it would be better if he could leave the general work to a deputy, and get on with the preparation of his own 'case', but Riddell certainly hadn't the qualifications to deputise. Bell? There was no report from Bell in the morning's accumulation, and that was unusual; it certainly did not mean that Bell had nothing to report. He put a call through to Bell's office.

"Mr. Bell's not been in this morning, sir."

"Hm," grunted Gideon. If he called Bell's home it would suggest either anxiety which wasn't really justified, or that he was checking up on him; Bell was too reliable a man for that. Gideon decided to wait. It was an unsatisfactory morning in every way, and he began to wish that he had not agreed to have lunch with Popple. He did not know Popple well, but knew nothing against him. The man had a lively sense of humour and a ready tongue, and some of his notices which had been sent round, about sport, pensions and other internal matters, had been quite lively. He had been in Fleet Street most of his life, and was now in the middle forties, a few years younger than Gideon.

They met in the front hall.

"Where are we going—the pub across the road?" asked Gideon.

The 'pub across the road' was in Cannon Row, and subsisted almost exclusively on hearty eating and long drinking men from the Yard.

"Not on your life, we're going to a slap-up place," said Popple, and reminded Gideon of Hopkinson; he was nearly bald, and had merry blue eyes, in a plump face set on an unexpectedly small body. "On the house, too. I don't often take VIPs out to lunch."

'What does he want?' wondered Gideon, cautiously.

They went to Quagg's, where the lunch was excellent, the atmosphere luxurious and the service almost unbelievable. Popple suggested wine, but Gideon stuck to lager; wine could make him heavy-eyed, and dull his wits. They had a table far away from others to make sure that they could talk without being overheard, and when they were waiting for their sweet, Popple said:

"Patient chap, Gideon, aren't you?"

"Wouldn't be much good at my job if I wasn't"

"No. What made you weigh into the Old Man like you did yesterday?"

"Who told you about it?"

"I picked it up."

"Hm." Gideon became very wary indeed, reminding himself that this was one of the Civil Staff, who might be trying to find out enough to report back to the Secretary; one could never be quite sure how a thing like this would go. "Well, I didn't weigh into the Old Man, I just made a plain statement of fact."

Popple grinned.

"That's one way of putting it. Needn't make a mystery out of it, I suppose, but I wanted to see how you'd jump. I happened to be in the Old Man's office yesterday afternoon, and there was a transcription of the notes which the Secretary had taken. What you had to say had been extracted verbatim. You set 'em all by the ears."

"Dare say," said Gideon, and he was still very wary.

"How much of it did you mean?" asked Popple.

"If I'd known you for years instead of one, I'd have your skin for that."

"Everything?"

"And more."

"Syd Taylor a case in point?"

"Yes."

"Heart and soul in this, George?" Popple had never

70

called him 'George' before. He was asking questions in quick succession, and watching Gideon very closely.

"I am."

"I could help," announced Popple.

The waiter came up with the fruit salad and a double ice-cream for Gideon, and pancakes for Popple. Gideon considered all this while the waiter hovered. Popple ordered 'coffee when we've finished', and waved the man away.

"How?" asked Gideon.

"Friends in Fleet Street could do a lot and I've a lot of friends," Popple answered. "I was told when I took this job on that the chief thing was to improve the public relationship—sell the Yard and the Force generally to the Press. You may not have noticed, but we get twenty per cent more space in the national dailies than we used to, and most of the extra is on the front page. Good, aren't I?"

"I'll tell you when I know."

Popple chuckled.

"Drop the defences, George. I'm not going to try and pull a fast one, I'm going to give you the opportunity you couldn't get if I wasn't on your side. It depends how much this business of economy cuts really matters to you. Were you serious when you said you'd be ready to drop down to super rank again?"

"Yes."

"Will you take other risks?"

"I might," said Gideon, cautiously. "What kind?"

"Unless something exceptional crops up, and I don't think it will, the Sunday papers will have very dull front pages this week," Popple told him. "They'll be made up tomorrow night, and short of an earthquake or a train disaster, they'll be full of froth. I could get three of them for certain if a highly placed officer at the Yard would state publicly that in his opinion the

71

Yard will be in Queer Street if more money and more men can't be found. If I said it, no one would really listen, it'd get a small paragraph at most, and I'd get a kick in the pants for indiscretion. But——"

Gideon just looked at him.

"You've never said much to the Press," Popple went on. "In fact I don't remember you being quoted for months. You needn't say much, either. The newspapers will tart it up for you." When Gideon continued to stare but didn't speak, Popple continued on as if a little embarrassed. "I'd broadcast it myself if I thought it would do any good, but I'm sure it wouldn't. I'm as sure you would. All you need say is what you've already said to the Old Man. You might hint that if the CID doesn't get an extra grant for staff and the renewal of equipment and installing more modern stuff, there'll be the biggest crime wave ever. I've got some new figures, just in," Popple added. "Last year's total of indictable offences in the Metropolitan area was up by—guess how much?"

Gideon said slowly: "Fifteen per cent."

"You psychic? Fourteen point seven per cent."

"I can add up, too."

"You can also make prophesies; you can prophesy to the Press that next year it will be up another twenty-five per cent, and the year after that thirty per cent, unless drastic steps are taken to increase recruitment, pay the present staff more, and—how many resignations from the Department did you have last year?"

"Seventeen," said Gideon. "Nothing to matter."

"Straws in the wind. They hated leaving but they've got wives and families."

Gideon sat very still, until he picked up his spoon again. The ice-cream had gone mushy. He put the spoon down and pushed the plate away. Conflicting thoughts were chasing each other in his mind, and he wanted time to think this out; on the other hand he realised that it might be now or never. He could see its enormous advantages. He had avoided seeking personal publicity since he had become Commander, for the men doing the work in the field needed it, but he was often named, and was quite sure that if he made a pronouncement it wold get good space in the newspapers. If Popple could get it on to ten million front pages on Sunday morning, it might be a big step towards rousing public opinion. One part of his mind was eager and willing, but there was a cold shadow of doubt in the other.

What would be the effect on the Commissioner?

If Scott-Marle resented it, what would he do?

It could not be dismissed as an indiscretion; no one would believe that Gideon would be so indiscreet. It would be a powerful shot in the battle he had started without meaning to. The Commissioner would almost certainly disapprove, strongly. On the other hand, there could not be a better opportunity, for the newspapers could play up the attack on Taylor and the escape of Micky the Slob.

He could refer the suggestions to Rogerson or to the Commissioner first.

They would say 'no', of course; neither could possibly agree that such a statement should be made.

If done, it would have to be wholly on his own responsibility, and he would have to be prepared to take all the consequences. He did not know the Commissioner well enough to be able to guess what they would be, but began to see the situation even more clearly. So far as the staffing position went in the CID, things could hardly be worse. Seventeen resignations in a year were not many, but they were a hundred per cent up on the previous year. This statement would attract mass attention, and even if he got a kick in the pants, might gain the extra money and the extra drive for new men.

The waiter came up with the coffee.

"Well, how about it?" Popple asked, when the man went off.

"How long can I have?" asked Gideon.

"Ten o'clock in the morning."

"Will you be in?"

"No, home. I'll contact you."

"Right."

"Mind telling me which way you lean?" asked Popple.

"Your way," Gideon answered, "but there may be snags in it that I can't see, and I don't mean snags for me. I'm due to prepare a case, anyhow."

"I know about that, but if you get your case you might find yourself up against another political crisis, or a revolt in East Europe, or—well, you know as well as I do," Popple said. "Ten million Sunday morning breakfast-tables at least, George—and you'll have your pretty picture on each of them."

"That's one of the things I'm afraid of," said Gideon.

They did not say much more, and Gideon gave Popple a lift back to the Yard. Once there, Gideon went up the stairs rather than in the lift, where he would probably have to talk to others. Head thrust forward and looking very massive, he made his way to his own office. He opened the door, deciding that the best thing he could do now was to get rid of Riddell for the afternoon, and then saw Joe Bell sitting at his, Gideon's desk.

His expression made it obvious that Bell had brought trouble.

"Taylor?" demanded Gideon.

"Yes," answered Bell. "He's gone. I happened to be there. So was his wife."

6

HEADLINES

Gideon had been known to say that when the machine of the Yard was properly geared, it would run itself; all it needed was oiling. There was some truth in this, although he did himself less than justice. It had been true during the day or two which followed the conference, for he had thought so much about Taylor and the staff problem that other matters, the routine oiling of the machine, had little more than cursory attention. By good fortune, it was a slack time; early summer often was. No big cases developed, either in London or the provinces, although three major arrests were made, each by a Yard man in the provinces, as the result of weeks of patient investigation.

Gideon did everything that had to be done mechanically that Friday afternoon, and left the office about half past five, reaching home soon after six o'clock. The two younger girls were home, but getting ready to go to their tennis club, and by half past six he was alone with Kate.

She was always surprising him; and she surprised him when she said quietly:

"Is Syd Taylor dead?"

"Good lord," said Gideon; and took her hands. "So you can really read me like a book."

"I can't think of anything else that would weigh on you like a ton," said Kate.

"I've something else weighing about ten tons," Gideon told her. "Let's go into the front room, I could do with a drink, and I'm not hungry yet. Had a smack-up lunch." He led the way, poured himself a stiff whisky, and Kate a gin and Italian. Then he told her the whole story of Popple's suggestion. He had not realised before how often he talked to Kate about the Yard's problems, although seldom about actual cases, but this was so much more than a problem of the Yard.

"If I do it, it really could be a boomerang," he said, "and it might not come to a question of resigning from Commander's rank. I might be demoted."

"What do you want to do?" asked Kate.

"If everything else was equal, I'd talk to the Press." When she didn't comment, Gideon went on: "But it's not so simple, Kate. We're really beginning to see daylight, financially, and——"

He was surprised to see her break into a smile.

"We have to live with ourselves, too. I don't see that you can do anything else but talk to this reporter, George."

"Sure it won't make too much difference to you if things should go wrong?"

"We managed on Chief Superintendent's pay for years, and they won't demote you lower than that," Kate said, still calm and practical. "But I've a feeling that it will work out all right." She half-persuaded him that she meant that. "What about the evidence that man-shortage is dangerous, dear? I suppose Taylor's death is all that's needed?"

"To make first impact, anyhow," Gideon agreed.

He remembered, then, that for a few unreal moments on the previous day, he had almost hoped that Taylor would die so as to ram home the truth of what he had said at the conference. He shook the self-reproach off, but it kept coming back. He felt it keenly next morning, a little after eleven o'clock, when Popple brought in a surprisingly youthful-looking man with the manner and fuzzy hair of a cartoon fanatic, who asked only three questions which mattered:

How long had Gideon felt like this? The answer was several years.

Did Gideon think that the murder of Detective Sergeant Taylor was a direct consequence of the shortage of men? Yes.

Did others in the CID share Gideon's anxiety?

"Don't bring any of the others into this," objected Gideon. "But if you want to get an idea of how many feel like it, ask a dozen senior officers who've retired in the last year or so."

"Good idea," the Fleet Street man said, and smiled as if he really thought it was. "Now, what about some personal details about your wife and family, and especially about this son of yours who wants to join the Force. Would you encourage him?"

Gideon wondered how a journalist had got that item of news. *Via* Popple?

"Not unless there's a reasonable chance that if he joins, the Force will have enough staff to cope."

"And how do you see the future of crime, Commander? Will it increase or decrease?"

"It will increase enormously if we aren't able to clap down on it, good and hard."

"And can I quote you as saying that?"

"Yes," answered Gideon, heavily.

Just before twelve o'clock, when the Fleet Street man and Popple had left, and he was in the office with Riddell, clearing up for the weekend, an urgent request came in from an east coast town for help in an investigation into a murder of a seven-year-old child. It was one of the nasty cases, although probably quite straightforward once the police had interviewed enough people, but the Bournsea killer was still at large. Almost certainly this story would be used by the Sunday newspapers as the current sensation to support what Gideon had said. There was nothing he could do about that, but it wasn't the real proof. They could have double the present CID strength but could not stop the occasional 'amateur' murder, the outbreaks of viciousness, the sex crime or the hate crime. These were not truly part of the war, but they would appear to be.

Gideon called in the Superintendent who had been to Bournsea, and told the telephone operator not to put calls through to him. He went into a small room, leaving Riddell to look after routine matters. Saturday midday was usually slack.

The Superintendent, a big, flat-footed man named Hill and nicknamed Hippo, was older than Gideon, a sound man of little imagination. He had a remarkable memory, and what was more rare, knew how to use it. His thick, straight hair was usually untidy, and today was no exception.

"What we have to find out is whether this could be tied up with the Bournsea job," Gideon said. "I know it's three hundred miles away, but there are a lot of similarities. Care to go up and have a look yourself, or rather send one of the chaps who worked with you?"

"Funny thing," Hill said, in a plummy voice, "the wife wanted a weekend by the seaside. I'm going to take her to Bournsea. Thought I might have a word with the coppers down there, as I happened to be on the spot. Pity to disappoint the wife, wouldn't it be?"

"We can't do that," said Gideon, already in a better

humour. "Like to send Evans to the east coast by himself, or take young Peto with him?"

"Send 'em both," advised Hill, promptly. "Bit of experience and ozone won't do either of them any harm. They won't need long, should be able to tell whether there's anything for us to work on in forty-eight hours. I can go up Monday if there's any need."

"Let's do it that way," agreed Gideon. "The Chief Constable's not one of the high-horse type, he won't mind being fobbed off with a DI."

"Can always tell him the CIs and the Superintendents on the cab-rank are up to their eyes," said Hill. "And that's not far wrong, either. I don't like complaining, George, but do you know how much holiday I've got due to me, last year and this?"

"Don't tell me."

"Six weeks."

"So you haven't really had a whole week off in eighteen months," said Gideon, heavily.

"That's right, and you ought to hear what the wife says about it. There are times when your name's mud. I told her that when you took on the job things would be better, see." He gave a grin, and his great jaws opened. "Nothing like a little joke, is there? Having any luck with the campaign, or is the Old Man regarding you as a bolshie?"

"Don't know yet," said Gideon.

'But I'll know after tomorrow morning's papers,' he thought, and made a pencilled note to check how many other men at the Yard and at the Divisions were going without holidays. Tired men couldn't do their best: that was another angle. Pity he hadn't thought about it while with the man from Fleet Street.

It was half past one before he had finished, but Saturday lunch was a movable feast. He stopped at the newspaper shop which still had the Bournsea crime poster on show, and ordered each Sunday newspaper to be delivered next day.

He wanted to be sure exactly what coverage he was given.

There was a match at the Oval he would have liked to see for the afternoon, but he owed the afternoon to Kate, and did not really regret missing his cricket. The whole family was home, all very bright, cheerful and noisy. Matthew rubbed salt in the minor wound by saying that he was going to scorch off to the Oval as soon as he could, the match he was to have played in this afternoon had been scratched. The girls had tennis on their minds, the youngest boys swimming. It was a medley of voices, laughs, retorts; as cheerful as a family could be, with Kate ruling it very quietly—and Kate with something on her mind.

When he had reached home, she had said: "Did you talk to that newspaper man?" and he'd answered: "Yes, given him the lot," and after that had realised that she hadn't asked for the sake of it. She went to do the washing-up, with the girls, and Gideon went upstairs to change into a pair of old flannels and a jacket; he planned to go round all the windows this afternoon, putting in new sash-cords and checking the blinds. He heard Kate coming up as he sat on the edge of their big double bed, lacing up a pair of paint-spotted old shoes which hadn't been cleaned for years.

"My turn for mind reading," he said, looking round and catching sight of three Kates: the real one and two reflections in the winged dressing-table mirror. "What's worrying you, dear?"

"I think you're going to hate it," Kate said.

"Oh, lor'." He hadn't the slightest idea what this presaged, unless it meant that Prudence wanted to advance the time of her marriage; she was planning to marry next Easter, but he had seen signs that her young man was not too happy about waiting so long.

"I tried to get you on the telephone, but they wouldn't put me through," Kate said. "It would have been difficult to talk about, anyhow." She was not often exasperating, like this. "It would probably have been too late, too—what time did you talk to the newspaper man?"

"Eleven." Then this was nothing remotely to do with Prudence. Gideon sat looking hard at Kate.

"I didn't get the invitation until a quarter to twelve," she said.

Gideon got up. "*What* invitation? What difference——"

"The Commissioner's wife rang up and asked if we would like to go and have lunch with her and the Commissioner tomorrow," Kate told him. "I didn't see how I could say no, because obviously he wants to talk to you away from the office. If I could have got you in time I'd have stopped you from talking to the Press, but you can't very well withdraw now, can you?"

"No, I can't," said Gideon, heavily. "God, what a blurry mess *that* makes." He caught a glimpse of his face in the mirror, and he had never looked so lugubrious; it almost made him grin. "Well, can't be helped, blast it. What did she say?"

"Not very much, really. She couldn't have been nicer, and I'm quite sure she wouldn't have invited us if the Commissioner really felt strongly against you."

"No," agreed Gideon. "Probably not."

Neither of them added the superfluous comment, that whatever was in the Commissioner's mind might be altered by tomorrow's headlines.

Gideon finished tying up his laces.

"Well, it'll be a damned good lunch, anyhow," he said. "Never got farther than a drink before, but I'm told the Old Man's a gourmet." Quite suddenly, he grinned: "Decided what you're going to wear?"

"I've decided that I was a fool not to have bought that hat last week," Kate said, "but I'm not going to go and rush out and get something that I'll probably hate in a week's time, so you'll have to take me in the best I've got. You ought to have had your blue suit pressed—I'll do that." She came and rested a hand on his shoulder. "I think perhaps she's much more human than you've ever realised, George."

"Might be," Gideon said. "All the same, I wish to heaven I'd kept my big mouth shut."

"Do you?" asked Kate, very quietly.

He looked at her steadily, and began to smile again. "You'll sing a different song when we're back on the bread-line," he said, and with a swift and quite irresistible movement he drew her down so that she was sitting beside him. "How about forgetting window-cords and ironing for the afternoon, and having a tumble——"

"*I've* got too much to do," Kate said firmly, but she didn't get up, and held his hand tight against her. "Anything else in, George?"

He didn't tell her about the east coast child murder; she hated crimes of that kind, and there was time enough to tell her tomorrow morning; then his own headlines would be enough for her to worry about.

He wondered what kind of a weekend it would be for crime; in general that 'war' of his. He found himself thinking that by calling it a war he had dramatised the whole issue, and others who were not so close to it as he might find it melodramatic. Then he shrugged gloom off, and wondered whether the two detectives now on their way to the east coast would find any con-nexion between that crime and the one at Bournsea.

Bournsea, like all seaside resorts, had a weekly exodus as well as a weekly influx of visitors. Saturday was the least-crowded day on the beach for the casual visitor, but they seldom realised it. The people who had been here for the week were on their way home, and new holidaymakers were still settling in at their hotels. Very few people who had seen the party of five children, the man and his dog during the week, were still there.

One or two Bournsea regulars noticed them; especially the man, the dog and the child who were strolling along the water's edge, towards one of the black groynes. Beyond this was an even less-frequented stretch of the promenade, and beyond this in turn, some little stretches of woodlands, beloved at night by courting couples and the promiscuous alike, but used very little by day. It was here that the dog ran, pouncing, after a ball which the man had tossed for him. The man and the child, hand-in-hand, were now on the promenade itself, and the other children were still in the water.

"Shall we go and help him find it?" the man asked. "Whoever finds it first can have *three* toffees."

"Oo yes, please," the child said, and actually tugged at his hand.

Five minutes later, she could not understand why he was holding her so tightly.

She was not really frightened . . .

The dog was chewing the sticky mass; that would keep him quiet for a long time.

* * *

Gideon woke a little after seven o'clock on the Sunday morning, lay with Kate sleeping by his side for ten minutes or so, and by that time could not stay any longer without fidgeting. The bed spring creaked as he got up. He ran his fingers through his hair, to flatten it, and rasped his hand over his stubble. Kate didn't look as if she would stir, so he went out. There was no sound from the children's rooms on this floor or upstairs. He looked down at the front door knowing that he would be lucky if the Sunday newspapers arrived before eight o'clock. He shaved, took his time bathing, and finished by twenty to eight. By then voices were sounding in the big attic floor room which he had partitioned for the boys years ago. Prudence came out of her bedroom, tying a dressing-gown round her. If her Peter had ever seen her like this, it was easy to understand why he was in a hurry; she was stretching and yawning, and looked lovely with sleep; and seductive. *His* daughter. She was wearing one of Kate's old nightdresses which had always been a size too small for Kate but was two sizes too large for Pru; and it gaped at the breast.

She was very, very lovely.

" 'Morning, Dad," she said, and suddenly became wide awake. She pulled up the neck of her dressing-gown hastily, and then went on: "Dad, can you spare me a minute?"

"Just going to make some tea," he said. "Come down and help me."

"I won't be a jiff, must pop into the bathroom," she answered.

It would be about advancing the date of the marriage, of course, and a wise parent ought to recognise the danger signals. Gideon had fought for a two years' delay, had won a year already, and Kate agreed that

85

this was the time to give in. Peter was a nice lad, too; almost certainly dependable.

But twenty-two seemed very young.

Was it?

Soon Pru came, so eager and so earnest, and full of logical argument. Peter wanted to take another job, he had to be married before he could get it, it meant two hundred pounds a year more; with a bit of luck they could even afford a small car, and *Mum* didn't mind, not really.

Gideon felt a little choky when he'd given way, and Prudence flung her arms round him with a passion which told him how lucky Peter was.

Then he saw that the newspapers were in the litter-box.

"Take the tea up to your mother, tell her I'll be up in a minute, and then go and get the others up," he ordered, gruff so as to hide his feelings. He strode to the door and took out four newspapers, all folded; opened the door and found the others on the porch. He gulped as he picked them up, then spread out the *Sunday Globe*, with a five million circulation, which the Fleet Street man had said was 'in the bag'.

Gideon almost winced.

CID CHIEF SAYS YARD LOSING BATTLE AGAINST CRIME

The *Echo* put it more simply:

CRIME ON THE UP AND UP—Yard Chief.

Gideon took the newspapers upstairs slowly, tucking several of them under his arm and looking at others in his hand. His photograph appeared in every one, a picture taken some years ago on a case; he looked ten years younger than he did today.

LONDON UNDER THREAT OF CRIME WAVE

another headline read, and a fourth:

SCOTLAND YARD LOSING TO CRIME

Prudence was coming out of the big bedroom, hurrying, but she stopped when she saw her father.

"You look as if you've lost a pound and found a penny," she said. "Has something happened during the night?" She glanced at the newspapers, and her eyes widened. "Gracious! Well you must have expected something to get all those. May I see?" She took a newspaper, and delight sprang into her bright eyes when she saw her father's picture. "My goodness they have done you proud! Mum," she went on, hurrying back into the bedroom, "Dad's hit the headlines at last. He looks like a cross between Jack Hawkins and Gregory Peck."

She went off with one of the newspapers, to carry the news to the rest of the family. Gideon spread the other papers out on the bed in front of Kate, who was sitting up; the tea tray was on a bedside table.

"That one has a circulation of three million," Gideon announced factually. "That one five, that one nearly two . . ." he estimated for each one, while Kate looked at him, not at the newspapers, and when he had finished, she said:

"Seventeen million copies."

"That what it adds up to?"

"Yes."

"Wonder if the classy ones have anything about it," Gideon asked aloud, and looked at the two smaller circulation newspapers, the kind which the Commissioner would be certain to read. "Here's the end column on the front page, no photograph though." He flipped over the pages of the other. "Middle page, and a profile," he said, and sat down heavily on an easy chair. "They've certainly gone to town on it, it'll take me all the morning to sort this lot out."

Kate was pouring tea.

Half an hour later, Gideon knew the gist of the different articles. In all but two, what he had said was connected with the murder of Syd Taylor; two mass-circulation newspapers had interviewed retired CID men, and in every case they were quoted as saying that the Yard had been seriously undermanned for at least twenty years.

Ever since the beginning of the Second World War the greatest police force and the greatest detective force in the world has been compelled to fight its own war with too few men and too few weapons. Government economy with the Criminal Investigation Department is criminal in itself.
It must not be permitted.

"Well," Kate said, an hour later, "it hasn't spoiled your appetite. Don't forget that you're going out to lunch today."

"If the Old Man doesn't cancel the invitation when he reads all this," said Gideon.

"No man could be such an utter lunatic," said Matthew.

That gave Gideon one supreme moment, for he saw the way his children looked at him, and sensed the hero worship of each one.

* * *

There was no mention in any of these newspapers of the seven-year-old girl, Rose Jeffson, who was missing from her home in Bournsea.

The local police knew about it, of course, but they assumed that the child had been drowned, and expected the body to be washed up on the beach before long.

Micky the Slob, hiding in the hold of a small tramp steamer due to sail for America the next morning, read the newspapers and saw himself mentioned in every one. He was no fool, and realised that the police would strain everything they could to get him.

Micky the Slob was frightened.

Among the other thirty-odd million people who read the story in one newspaper or another was Keith Ryman. He was sitting in his small flat in Mayfair, with the newspapers spread out about him, when his 'wife', a blonde as pretty as could be, cuddly, and dressed as if Hartnell had made her clothes, came in from the bedroom to the chair where he sat looking through a large window over Hyde Park.

"Sure you won't come out with me, darling?"

"Too lazy," Ryman said, smiling at her; his eyes crinkled attractively when he smiled. "You take Flossie for her exercise, I'll be ready to take you out to lunch when you get back."

"All right." Helen Woodley, who called herself Helen Ryman, kissed him lightly on the forehead and went out, calling her French poodle from the bedroom. Ryman waited for the door to close, and waited again until he saw Helen walking across Park Lane, towards the park. Then he stretched out and dialled a Mayfair number, and was answered at once.

"Come and see me, Rab, will you?" he asked.

"Right away, Keith. Wouldn't have anything to do with a certain front-page story, would it?"

"Wouldn't it?" Ryman smiled as he replaced the receiver. He leaned back, put his folded hands beneath his head, and looked up at the sky. "Hit 'em hard and often in five or six places at the same time, and then do the real job when they're not expecting it. That's the strategy all right."

He took his hands from the back of his neck, and rubbed them together.

7

LUNCHEON

"Well, hold your breath," Gideon said.

He had parked the car a few doors away from Scott-Marle's house in Radlett Square, one of the smaller, lesser known and more exclusive of London's squares; it was still residential. There was a small green patch in the middle of it, with a few plane trees, some rhododendron bushes and some laurel. One or two dogs were playing, two nursemaids were sitting on a wooden bench with a pram by each. On another seat were boy and girl—lovers.

Gideon saw all of this without appearing to notice it, as he armed Kate up the short flight of stone steps which led to Scott-Marle's house. The front door was painted black, and the knocker and the letterbox looked like solid silver.

"At least we've the same colour scheme," Kate remarked.

Gideon said: "I'll bet he didn't do any of the painting himself," and pressed the bell.

He was dressed in a suit, bought at Kate's insistence last year, which served him for many formal daytime occasions; it was nearly black, had a very narrow grey stripe, and was beautifully cut and made by a little Jewish tailor who worked in the East End and had known Gideon for many years. He looked and felt spruce and almost too much at his best. During the moment or two that they waited, he looked Kate up and down. She had on a bluey-green silk suit, perhaps a trifle easy fitting, for she hated her clothes to be too tight, and a hat to match—she had trimmed it herself with the same material as the suit.

"What's the matter, I look all right, don't I?" she asked urgently; for he seldom looked at her so intently.

"You look"—he hesitated, and then let the word come—"just right. Don't alter a thing."

She squeezed his hand.

The door was opened, almost without a sound, by a young footman, bandbox dressed. Hardly had the effect of this unaccustomed formality touched the Gideons when Lady Scott-Marle came hurrying from a big room with double doors. She could not be much more than thirty, and her husband was undoubtedly in his late fifties. She was tall but not so tall as Kate, between colours, and strikingly attractive. She wore a suit of pale grey with white spots, and Kate could not have been more suitable dressed.

"Hallo, Mrs Gideon, I've so often wanted to meet you, and I've heard so much about your husband." She had blue eyes, the merry kind. "Do come along in."

Gideon was handing his hat and gloves to the footman, and wondering how the subject heaviest on his mind would come up. Would Scott-Marle's tactics be to talk on trivialities before and during the meal? Socially, that would be right, but Gideon hoped that there would be a way of avoiding a long delay, although he must not break the ice himself.

The hall was small, and he did not notice much about it, except two portraits, the circular staircase, and the passage alongside. The room into which Scott-Marle's wife took them was much larger than he had expected, high-ceilinged, with a beautiful double bay window overlooking an unexpected garden, vivid with wallflowers and tulips, forget-me-not and polyanthus. All this Gideon saw as one takes a photograph. There was the black grand piano, the Regency style of décor and furniture, and the Commissioner, moving forward from the fireplace, which Gideon knew was Adam.

Scott-Marle was dressed in a black and white overcheck suit; not exactly sporting, not really formal; and on the instant Gideon felt overdressed. Thank God Kate wasn't.

Scott-Marle was shaking her hand.

Then he was taking Giedon's.

His wife was so vital, her complexion so good, and vivacity showed in every movement she made, even in the turn of her head. Scott-Marle was rather dried-up, like his Greek gods. He was tall, too thin, almost hollow-cheeked, with a touch of tan which gave the impression that he was suffering from jaundice. His hair was cut very close to a somewhat narrow head, and suddenly he was a personality, and not remote at all.

He did not open his mouth when he spoke; nor even when he smiled.

"What's it like to have a husband in all the headlines, Mrs Gideon?" His tone could almost be called bantering.

Gideon thought: 'Thank God, he's out with it,' and immediately felt acutely anxious for Kate, so tempering his own relief.

"Darling, let them have a drink first," Lady Scott-Marle protested.

Damn' nice woman; she saw that Kate was on the spot.

Kate was smiling at the Old Man.

"It's the first time it's happened since I've known him," she said; "it's rather a thrill." Her smile was spontaneous, and Gideon, who knew the sign, felt a moment of panic; she hadn't finished yet and there was going to be a barb in what she added: "Now it has happened, I hope that someone's going to sit up and take notice."

Gideon had never heard the Commissioner laugh before. He actually opened his mouth wide.

It was an excellent meal; Gideon had never tasted duck and green peas cooked to such perfection, and there was a creamy sweet, a confection which reminded him of something he'd had in Switzerland, years ago; finally there were coffee and cigars, and Gideon found himself in a small first-floor study, overlooking the back garden, where Kate was going round with Lady Scott-Marle; Kate was the Gideon gardener.

They had touched only lightly on Yard affairs, and the only thing Gideon could feel sure about was that his Boss was not going to be on his dignity, or vengeful about the newspaper story. Now he sat down, pulling at the cigar as if it were a pipe; Scott-Marle stood with his back to the window.

"Why don't you throw that away and fill your pipe?" Scott-Marle said. "I'm sure you'd prefer it." Gideon did. "Now I'd like to have your considered view of the staff situation," Scott-Marle went on, "without any need to fight or argue with the other departmental heads. You know as well as I do that there'll always be some feeling between the various departments, and the CID certainly gets the plums in publicity. Did the Taylor business make you talk to the Press?"

That was as safe an explanation as any; and being partly true, it helped.

"A newspaper man caught me just after I'd heard," Gideon said, "and I was so mad . . ." He talked a little more; and then found himself rationalising his approach. Syd Taylor was only one factor. "We're stretched far too thin, that's the truth of it, and have been for years. There aren't even enough allowances made for sickness and holidays. Hill, on the Bournsea child murder case, has actually taken his wife there so that she can get a weekend's holiday, and . . ." He quoted a dozen cases, and also explained what he had done on Friday in the Divisions. "I think that probably stamped on anything planned for the weekend, but sooner or later one of us is going to miss something he would see if he weren't so busy."

"Do you mean, someone will organise a wave of crime?"

"I don't think any of the old hands will try to organise anything on a big scale, we'd have had a lot of squeaks by now," Gideon answered. "But most of these people we deal with are imitative. We get a crop of smash and grabs, a crop of fine art thefts, a crop of holdups, an outbreak of shoplifting—it seems to go in waves." Gideon was really warming up. "Micky the Slob's killed Taylor, it's all over the newspapers—and you can take it from me that before the week's out two or three more policemen or detectives will be attacked, because some swine will argue that if Micky can get away with it, so can they."

Scott-Marle said: "Won't today's newspapers encourage them still more?"

Was that a criticism?

"Probably," Gideon answered.

"Then there's a risk that the stories do more harm than good."

"Of course there is," Gideon agreed. "The newspapers are telling them today what Micky the Slob told them yesterday, but that'll only have a short-term effect. We can go after them with all we've got, and smack 'em down for a few weeks. Its the long-term situation that worries me. We don't have enough men even to send to the provinces, and Hill and his two chaps ought never to have come back from Bournsea. I haven't laid it on too thickly, Commissioner, take my word for that."

"I do," the Commissioner answered him. "Rogerson agrees with you absolutely, and so do two or three of the other department heads. But all of them need extra money and more men, especially the uniformed branch, even if the most urgent need is in your department. I'm now practically convinced, but——"

Gideon interrupted, warmly: "You don't know what a relief it is to hear that."

"I hope I'm not misleading you," said Scott-Marle, and Gideon sensed something which hadn't yet been said. "You may have convinced me, but that's a very different thing from convincing the Home Office and the Treasury. I had two calls from the Home Secretary this morning. He's not at all happy about the newspaper stories, which he says look like a deliberate attempt to force the hand of the Government."

Gideon realised how justified that was the moment it was said, and felt suddenly, badly, shaken.

Scott-Marle hadn't finished.

"Other people will probably resent it, too," he went on. "Every department and all the services are being axed, and in my view the best you'll get is *status quo*. Even that won't be easy."

"If you're with us, we've surely a chance of getting a bit extra," Gideon said, trying to ward off depression.

"It may be worth trying," the Commissioner conceded. "I want you to concentrate on this problem for a few weeks. Delegate as much of your normal work as you can and find the evidence that I can take to the

Minister, with reasonable hope of making the case unanswerable. I'll arrange for Popple to give you all the help he can. I needn't advise you not to overdo the Press interview business now," Scott-Marle went on, "but Popple can probably slant a lot of stories your way to show the situation as you've presented it. I'll arrange for one of our legal department to work with you, too, as well as someone from the Secretary's office. If I take this case to the Minister, I've got to convince him. If I can do that, he'll fight for us. Even then it'll be a toss-up whether he or the Chancellor of the Exchequer wins. What we need is an unanswerable case."

He stopped.

Gideon said, very gruffly: "You'll get it, sir."

"Good!" Scott-Marle tapped the end off his cigar at last, and stood up, to glance out of the window. Kate and Lady Scott-Marle were swinging gently in the garden seat. "Do you go in much for gardening?"

"My wife——" Gideon began, a little awkwardly because of the deliberate change of subject. He was glad when the telephone bell rang.

"Sorry," said Scott-Marle, and lifted the receiver. "Scott-Marle here . . . Yes, he's with me at the moment, hold on." He handed the instrument to Gideon, who was astonished; only the family knew where to find him, and this would make it look as if he had spread the invitation news around, would make it look as if he couldn't keep his mouth shut. "Who's that?" he asked, abruptly.

"Daddy, it's Penny," said his second daughter, a little breathlessly. "I know you said no one was to ring, but Superintendent Hill rang up, he said he'd tried to get you at the Yard, and must speak to you. I asked him where he was, and he said Bournsea Police Headquarters. I promised to tell you as soon as I could, but I was right not to give him the number, wasn't I?"

"Absolutely right, Penny." Gideon was delighted and yet anxious at the same time. "I'll call him right away, see you soon." He rang off, looked at Scott-Marle, and said: "That was my daughter. I don't much like the sound of this, Hill wants to talk to me urgently. May I call him at Bournsea?"

"Let me put the call in for you," Scott-Marle said; and to Gideon's surprise, was able to give the Bournsea number from memory. "Yes, ring me as soon as you get Superintendent Hill on the line." He put down the receiver, and added, to Gideon: "I hope this isn't another child murder."

"George," said Hippo Hill, "we've found another seven-year-old girl, same circumstances as the other job down here. Can you get Evans and Peto down from Scarborough, and let me have a team? . . . With all these holidaymakers here we're going to have a hell of a lot of trouble."

"I'll send you a team," Gideon promised, "and I'll get it down to you tonight."

"There's a pal."

"Anything to go on?"

"Well, as a matter of fact, one queer thing," said Hill. "You remember the first case, there were some marks on the girl's clothes which looked as if they'd been made by a dog's paws, and there was some dog's spittle on her right hand? Same traces of spittle and of a toffee on this child's. Wouldn't like to let that news out yet, but we're going to start looking for a man with a dog. . . . Hell of a case in its way, the mother goes out to work, and we've lost a day because everyone thought it was missing by drowning until a couple going for a cuddle on the grass found the kid. . . . Yes, and strangled."

Gideon said: "Pull out all the stops, Hippo. We've got to get that swine quick."

He rang off.

Scott-Marle was watching intently.

"We could do with two hundred and fifty men extra down there," said Gideon, and that did not sound extravagant as he said it. "If that was the only job they did for a month, it would be worth it to make sure the swine doesn't get a third victim."

"You've already convinced me that you're right," the Commissioner said, quietly. "Why don't you go over to the Yard at once? I'll run your wife home—or my wife will—and I'll have a word with the Chief Constable at Bournsea."

Keith Ryman first heard about the Bournsea crime on the television that afternoon. A photograph of the dead child was flashed on the screen, with a police request for anyone who had seen a man with her to inform the nearest police station.

". . . over a hundred policemen are engaged in the hunt for clues," the announcer said.

Ryman snapped his fingers.

"What's the matter, honey?" Helen asked.

"Just thinking," Ryman replied. "Just had an idea."

8

MASS ATTACK

Gideon did his share of the investigation from his desk,
but he knew exactly what was happening in Bournsea.

It was as if a great animal had woken, shrugged himself and begun to prowl. In Bournsea itself, and in the
county surrounding it, messages went out to all police,
uniformed or plain-clothes branch, on duty or off. As
it was Sunday, the weekend traffic going away from the
seaside resort was very heavy, but except at key points
the uniformed police were taken off traffic control, and
special constables and AA and RAC scouts took over.

It was a fine day, with the temperature about seventy
degrees, although as usual the sea temperature was ten
degrees or more lower. The beaches were crowded.
There were masses of weekenders and more day trippers, but if the police drive was left until tomorrow,
when the crowds would be smaller, then anyone who
had been here last evening might be gone, and be almost impossible to trace; people were notoriously reluctant to come forward in response to police requests.

Everyone on the beach had to be questioned.

Had they been there between five and seven o'clock
yesterday?

Had they seen the five children? The one child, at the sea's edge? A dog? A man?

The police worked from the main pier towards the wooded land where the child's body had been found buried under clumps of bush and bracken. That area was now cordoned off, yet almost besieged by holiday-makers, girls in briefs and youths in loincloths, the very young, the middle-aged and the elderly. All went to gape. A party of police, thirty strong, was going over the two-acre patch of woodland very closely, for the girl's hair-ribbon had come off somewhere between the beach and the murder-spot. They looked for anything else which might be a clue, for footprints, for the paw-prints of the dog, and for any apparently trifling thing which might help them to build up the case.

Of course there were the newspaper men, including a dozen photographers.

Hill was in immediate charge of the search, and a tall, lantern-jawed Bournsea Superintendent named Appleton was constantly with him.

The General Post Office had been opened and emergency staff brought in, to check and list everyone who had a dog licence. The records were kept alphabetically; they had to be divided into districts, then lists had to be drawn up and attached to ward maps; very soon the search was likely to narrow down to a specific dog. Then with luck, someone who had seen the man and the dog would be able to give the police a recognisable description.

On the telephone to Hill, who had arranged with the GPO engineers to rig him up a kind of field telephone on the spot, Gideon said:

"Don't forget to tell your chaps to look out for dead dogs—drowned or buried or burnt. If this chap gets to know we're looking for a dog, he isn't likely to be very sentimental. Might be easier in the long run to trace a man who had a dog which has disappeared, than to do it the hard way."

"I won't forget," Hill said.

"How are things down there?"

"Appleton's having kittens, he's afraid that if there's much more of a scare, it might frighten families away from the place for their holidays. His Watch Committee's on his tail, and the local Publicity Officer seems to think that all will be ruination. The local Hotel Association is putting on the pressure, too."

"Anything else we can do for you from here?"

"Can't say there is," Hill answered, as if reluctantly. "It can't be for long, but we've all the men we can use today. If we pick the chap up by tonight, we can pat ourselves on the back."

"Any ideas at all?" Gideon urged.

"There are forty-seven thousand residents in Bournsea and there were an estimated twenty-five thousand holidaymakers on Saturday, and I haven't a clue of any kind," said Hill, very deliberately. "No one's come forward, no one's been found to admit seeing the man, the child and the dog. But it's early yet, not quite five o'clock."

"I'll be at home if you want me," Gideon said.

"Some people have the luck," quipped Hill, and then actually chuckled. "There's one thing, my wife's decided to stay down here for the next week at least."

"Tell her to enjoy herself," Gideon made himself say.

He rang off, spent ten minutes going through all the cases in hand, then left the office, and walked through the nearly deserted building, down to his car. So far, everything else was quiet, the crop of arrests and warnings given by the Divisions was still paying off.

Would it, for long?

"I can understand the holiday town's feelings," said Kate, when he got home, complaining. "I wouldn't like to be down on the beach with the children young again. It's bad enough wondering if they're going to drown. To feel that you'd have to watch them on the sand and promenade as well—it would spoil the holiday for me, and for any mother, I should think."

"That's what they're afraid of," Gideon said. "Did the Old Man tell you anything about his attitude to the staff problem after I'd left?"

"He didn't say anything in so many words, but he let me know it was all right with him." Kate was sitting comfortably in an easy chair, her feet up on a pouffe; it was nearly six o'clock. From the front room came the music of piano and violin; Prudence was a violinist in the BBC Symphony Orchestra, and Penelope hoped to become a professional pianist. "I couldn't believe you really had anything to worry about, George. He was quite human, wasn't he?"

"Very."

"She was charming, too," said Kate, and her eyes reminiscently lit up.

That luncheon visit was going to linger in her mind for a long time to come, but Gideon gave it very little thought; his mind was grappling with the main problem, with the need to appoint someone who could stand-in for him, with anxiety for word from Bournsea, and with that other more vague anxiety which he could not really name but which was there; that the Yard had reached danger-point on the matter of manpower, and that if there were a crop of major crimes it would be very difficult to cope. He kept telling himself that he might be over-anxious, that it was an inverted kind of wishful thinking; but at heart he was sure that he had

103

been anxious about the situation for a much longer time than he had realised; the last few days had simply brought it out.

If Hill could finish down in Bournsea in a day or two, it would help.

Gideon had a bad moment, then. His main thought was for Hill and the investigation and its effect on the Yard generally, not for the murdered child's mother, or for the general anxiety that so many others felt. This was a factor which he hardly realised existed; the domination of the importance of the job as a job, the organisation for its own sake, over the human factors. Once human understanding and sympathy were blunted, one stopped being a good policeman.

Another George, George Arthur Smith, was on the crowded beach at Bournsea, without his dog; the dog was behind the small corner shop, where he lived with his widowed mother, a very frail old lady who just managed to keep shop and home going. He was not thinking of his mother or the dog as he saw the policeman in uniform and the big men in plain-clothes going from person to person, threading their way over buckets and spades, past deckchairs, sand-castles, little rivers of water running down to the sea, past beach-huts, bathing attendants, the whole colourful variety of the seaside.

George Arthur Smith was rather a small man, very tanned because he spent a great deal of his time on the beach. He saw the crowd at the approach to the woodland, but did not go near it. He saw a big, ugly man approaching him, and felt a tremor of anxiety, but it did not go very deep.

"Sorry to bother you, sir," the man greeted. "I'm from the police. Are you a local resident?"

"Yes," answered Smith.

"Were you on the beach yesterday, about half past four onwards?"

"No," said Smith. "I was here a little earlier than that, but not at half past four."

"Did you notice a child playing alone at the edge of the sea?"

"I dare say I saw twenty children playing there," Smith answered, and managed to smile. "I'm afraid I don't take much notice of children, though, being a bachelor. I just came for a swim as I do most Saturdays and Sundays."

"I see, sir. Did you notice a child playing with a dog?"

Smith stared at him without the slightest change of expression for a moment, and then his lips twisted in a kind of smile, and he replied:

"There were several dogs, there usually are, but the only one I noticed was a bulldog. What kind of dog do you mean?"

"I'd like to know about any kind you saw playing with a child," the detective said.

"I can't honestly say that I remember anything like that," said Smith, frowning, as if with the effort of concentration. "And I'd left the beach after my swim by half past three, my mother—I live at home you see—wanted some shopping done, and I always do the shopping for her. I must have been home for tea at five o'clock." He shrugged, as if that disposed of the question.

His interrogator said: "Thank you for your frankness, sir, you may have been a great help. May I have your name and address?"

Inwardly, Smith's heart was pounding.

Outwardly, he was very calm.

"Why, what good will that do?"

"It's often helpful if we can compare two lots of evidence, sir." The detective was not looking at Smith, but at two plain-clothes men some distance away, who were talking to an elderly woman; she was pointing down to the sea's edge. "Something you saw may give someone else's memory a jerk, or something they saw might help yours. It's not likely we'll need to worry you, sir, but we might."

Smith said, reluctantly: "Well, I suppose that's reasonable. My name is Sanderson, and I live at"—there was the merest moment of hesitation before he went on—"17 Brindle Street. That's the big estate at the back of the town."

"I know Brindle Street." The detective wrote the name and address down, nodded briskly, then went to join the elderly woman, who was pointing again; quite a crowd had gathered round her and the plain-clothes men.

She was saying: "It was a big dog, a bit of a setter but with a spaniel's ears and face, browny-red in colour, but not a *bright* red like a red-setter. It wasn't yesterday but the day before I saw them. The little girl was frightened of the dog, and the man was reassuring her. I thought it was very nice of him to take the trouble. You don't think——"

"Could you describe the man, madam?" the detective asked.

Smith, just within earshot, stared out to sea and inwardly cursed a child near by who was crying.

". . . didn't really see him, I'm rather short-sighted, you see. The dog was racing about, and it came quite close to me, but the man . . ."

Smith did not hurry away, but walked past the mob of sightseers, saw a big man with a big, heavy jaw not far along, then took the short cut to the town that he usually did. He reached the shop, a mile away from

106

Brindle Street, a little after six-thirty. He heard Nicky, his dog, frisking in the kitchen. He went in, and the dog leapt at him, licking his face, pawing his clothes; his voice was sharper than usual when he told it to get down. His mother was out; she was at chapel, and would not be back until nine o'clock or after, for she always went to friends for supper after the service. Smith went to the back of the shop premises, and lit a fire in the hot-water boiler, a small grey stove.

The dog sat and watched him.

Then Smith went to a small shed, took down a tin plainly marked *Poison*, and carefully shook some of the lumpy white contents on to his hand. He hesitated, and watched the dog staring up at him, head on one side, tail wagging slowly, obviously asking for a walk.

"Won't be long," Smith said. "We'll go down to the beach. That's right! Down to the beach!"

The dog waved its tail vigorously.

Smith went back to the kitchen, opened a small packet of dog food, and tossed one or two crunchy pieces to the dog; each time, the piece went deep into its throat, and he hardly troubled to chew.

Then Smith tossed the potassium cyanide.

The bones didn't matter; he could always bury the bones.

At half past ten that night, Hippo Hill telephoned Gideon. Two people had seen a dog answering the same description, a cross between a spaniel and a red-setter, one on Thursday, one on Friday—no one had seen it on Saturday, so far as the police could find out.

"And neither of them can describe the man who

talked to the child," Hill said. "It's going to be a long job, George."

"That's what I was afraid of," Gideon said, glumly.

About the same time, a few miles away from Hurlingham, Keith Ryman was at the bar of a little Mayfair night club. His Helen was dancing on a small floor, and Ryman, there with a party of eight, was talking to Rab Stone. The atmosphere was surprisingly clear and clean. The police had never attempted to close this club up, for as West End clubs went, it was as clean as a whistle, and it gave reasonably good value. The only fact which had ever interested the police was that occasionally tricksters and vice men came here, but the types could be found anywhere, and there was no regular clientele of that kind.

No police watchers were here tonight.

Ryman was saying, very quietly: "I told you before and I'll tell you again, Rab, this is the time all right. Hit 'em hard in four or five places at once, to distract them, and then stage the big show. And there's a sure-fire way of distracting them just now."

"What way?"

"We want to pick up a couple of kids—like the Bournsea job."

Stone exclaimed: "Gawd?"

"Don't you like the idea?" Ryman glanced round, to make sure that no one was within earshot.

"It would work all right," Stone agreed.

"Can you get the job done?"

"I dare say," Stone said, "but——"

"Getting cold feet?" Ryman demanded.

"It's not that, Keith, but I wouldn't like anything to happen to kids."

"Of course we can't kill any kids, we don't want to

be caught on a murder rap, but we could snatch two or three, couldn't we?" Ryman said. "There's that case up in Scarborough, in the papers this morning. Kids are always being kidnapped, and it won't do them any harm if they're not hurt. Only got to feed 'em for a day or two."

Stone was still uneasy.

"It might be difficult, Keith, I don't know anyone who could handle that kind of job." When a man came up to the bar, he stopped talking and sipped his drink. Helen passed again, still grimacing; the stout man had her tightly in his arms. Ryman and Stone moved farther away from the bar.

"I could lay on holdups, smash and grabs, even——"
He broke off.

"Don't tell me you've got an idea," said Ryman, a little sardonically.

"There's something good we *could* lay on," said Stone, so softly that Ryman could only just hear him. "We could fix one or two attacks on coppers, that always draws 'em—like wasps round a honey-pot they are if one of their own chaps gets hurt. I was talking to Si Mitchell this morning—we were having a pint together—about that copper who was killed. Si was saying there were one or two coppers he'd like to dig a grave for. Now we could work out something on that, Keith, find two or three chaps who've got it in for the coppers and fix it up." He was talking as the thoughts entered his mind, and there was a glitter in his eyes; and there was a sharp interest in Ryman's. "Why not two one day, two the next? Different parts of London, too. Keith, that's a stroke of genius, that is—an absolute stroke of genius!"

"Could be," Ryman conceded.

"Don't be modest, it was really your idea, I've only dressed it up a bit. One in the East End, say, one right on the doorstep here—Soho, I mean, not this doorstep—why not come out Greenwich way, and another to Hammersmith or Ealing. Each job would be done by a different individual, that's the beauty of it. Even if the cops got all four, they couldn't trace it back to us. All we do is to get Si to——"

"It'll take some working out," Ryman interrupted, an edge of excitement in his voice. "I'd say we'd better do a job with two coppers and two kids, but you may be right. The only important thing is to get it laid on properly, so that the cops are stretched so tight they'll snap if they get another big job. Rab, we're on to something, and when you come to think about it, it's damned funny. Gideon of the Yard gave us the idea!"

Stone laughed, immoderately.

The music stopped, and Helen disentangled herself from the fat man except for her hand; he held on to it tightly. The two couples on the floor headed for tables or the bar.

"What about Helen, is she going to be okay?" Stone asked, checking his laughter.

"Don't worry about Helen," Ryman said. "Do you know what she's got for a heart?"

"I give up."

"A diamond, Rab, that's all, a bloody great diamond. And she wants to get bigger-and-bigger-hearted every day!"

"So long as you can trust her."

"I can trust her with everything except thinking, if she has to think, she gets in trouble," Ryman said, and stretched out his hands for his Helen; the stout man relinquished her with obvious reluctance, and gave a jerky bow. Helen took Ryman's hand, and looked up at him with beautiful eyes; eyes which really looked starry, and on which the eye shadow hardly showed.

"He was *beastly*, darling, do I have to be nice to him any more?"

"He's a very wealthy man," Ryman told her, solemnly.

"It looks as if it would take dynamite to separate him from any of his wealth," Helen said.

"Just a beautiful woman, my pet!"

"Well, next time he wants to dance with me, tell the band to make it a quickstep. Even he couldn't get that hold with a quickstep." Helen squeezed Ryman's fingers. "Are we going to stand at the bar all night, or are you coming to the table?"

She led the way to the table.

"Rab," said Ryman on the telephone next morning, "Helen's going out to Elstree. She thinks she may have a part. How about coming round for a drink? Twelve o'clock, say. Don't try anything on Si yet, let's give it plenty of thought. There's no hurry."

"You seen the morning papers, too?" Rab Stone asked, and laughed. "Okay. I'll be there."

Gideon had been in his office for two hours when Stone and Ryman made their appointment, and for one of these hours had been preoccupied with the Bournsea job. There had been no further developments, and there was no reasonable hope of quick results. The visit to every householder who held a dog licence was being planned; in Bournsea and the surrounding district from which bathers at the beach could be drawn, there were eleven thousand dog licences.

"And then you always got the so-and-so's who are too mean to pay for a licence," Hill said. "Half this town's so spread out, with a long drive to every house, that it'll take a week to cover it, and then only if nothing else happens. Not that we're likely to get another murder, unless we're dealing with a madman, and he strikes again while the hunt's on. Cheerful, aren't I?"

"Just keep at it," Gideon encouraged.

He rang off, and saw Riddell tapping his mouth as he yawned; Riddell had admitted having a late night, and had been working at half pressure all the morning. The others were still away, one with his flu and the other on the second week of his holiday. Gideon could recall the man from holiday, but knew that he badly needed a rest.

Two telephones rang on Riddell's desk.

"Always thought these office jobs were cushy," he grumbled as he lifted one and said: "Hold on," and then turned to the other and said: "Commander Gideon's office. . . . Yes, Riddell speaking . . . *What?*"

He bellowed the last word; and for the first time Gideon saw him really excited.

"Hold on," he said explosively, and his eyes glowed as he stared at Gideon. "It's Bell. They've cornered Micky the Slob on a Dutch cargo boat—Customs chaps found him. He's locked himself in a cabin, says he'll set fire to the boat if we don't give him a chance. Bell says all our River chaps and all the men we can spare are needed for the job. Micky means what he says."

9

THE CYNIC

A cordon of dock police was thrown round the berth where the Dutch vessel *van Doorn* was tied up. The crew had been taken off, except for the captain and two engineers, and were in a group some distance away, watching. Fifty police were at different vantage-points about the docks, all of them prepared for the one thing which was always possible with Micky the Slob: outside interference from his friends. Someone was almost certain to cause a distraction so as to give him a chance of getting away.

There could be very little chance.

Six launches of the Thames Division were drawn up in a fairly narrow semicircle about the *van Doorn*, which was hardly more than a coasting vessel, bringing fruit and vegetables across the North Sea from The Hague. Each launch was manned by four members of the River Police, and several smaller motor boats, cruising up and down, were ready to make sure that no one could get aboard the *van Doorn*. Every man present knew that Micky the Slob could not escape this time, and every man had a picture of Syd Taylor in his mind's eye.

Yet there was fear that he might yet fool them.

In charge of the Divisional Police was Hopkinson of NE Division, and he knew the docks as well as he knew his own home. With the care of a military commander, he had blocked every possible escape route.

Bell was also there.

"Now what we've got to decide is whether to send a raiding party, or whether to starve him out," Hopkinson said.

"What do you want to do?" asked Gideon, into the telephone.

"Raid."

"Is he armed?"

"I don't know for certain, but I expect so."

"Is it easy to get to the cabin where he's hiding?"

"It's at the foot of a small gangway, and he's barricaded the doorway," Hopkinson said. "He's got some tins of petrol down there, and says that if we go down again he'll toss petrol out, and start a fire. He knows he'll hang for Taylor, of course, and doesn't care which way he dies. But we can't afford to have him stand us off again, George, he'll have everyone in London laughing his head off at us."

"Right," said Gideon. "You got the fire service there yet?"

"No."

"I'll lay it on," said Gideon, "and I'll lay on a couple of fireproof suits, too. We want a volunteer from the fire-fighting units, someone who really knows how to deal with a fire if it starts, and a volunteer from your chaps."

"Hopkinson."

"You keep out of it," Gideon ordered. "That's an order—don't go down that gangway. We can't risk losing top men. Can't you get a volunteer?"

"I can get dozens," Hopkinson said. "I suppose you're right. How's the big war going?"

"All right," said Gideon.

He rang off, and immediately called the Superintendent who maintained a close liaison with the fire-fighting service, especially on all matters relating to arson. He made all the necessary arrangements, rang off, and had a few minutes of respite. Riddell kept glancing across at him. On Gideon's desk were the usual reports, and he had not yet briefed half of the officers on the cases which had hung over from last week, or had cropped up this weekend. It would take fully two hours, and he had never felt less like working on that job.

Riddell said out of the blue: "You know your trouble, don't you?"

Gideon was astonished.

"Trouble? What's that?"

"You haven't grown up," said Riddell, looking almost smug. "Still wish you were a copper on the beat—you'd rather be going down that gangway than anyone else, wouldn't you?"

Gideon was surprised into a laugh.

"Perhaps you're right," he conceded, and leaned back in his chair, massive, tie hanging down, shirt open at the neck, grey hair a little untidy. Under his hand were the records of criminals and crimes both small and big, wife-beaters, drunks, pickpockets, shoplifters, small-time vice racketeers; organised prostitution, fraud, rape; requests from two men to be extradited, one from France, one from Germany. There were recommendations for arrest, recommendations for investigation into the activities of private companies, three pending prosecutions for customs offenses, the beginning of a big probe into currency forgeries, with slush being produced either in England or just across the Channel. His job was to bring his great experience to bear on all of these things, to consider each and to advise the men who were doing the work of investigation: yet Riddell was right, he would give his right arm to be the Divisional man who volunteered to go aboard the *van Doorn*. "Didn't know you were a big thinker," Gideon went on, and there was only a touch of malice in his words.

Riddell sniffed.

"Lot of things about me you don't know," he retorted. "I don't believe in keeping my nose to the grindstone like you do. Perhaps it's my conscience that's wrong. But for twenty years I've been in the Yard, and I've never known the time when we ever had a fair break. Supposed to dedicate our whole lives to it, that's what you say, in effect—and *you* do it. So do a few others, but there aren't many."

"If you're going to use the word 'dedicated', nine of our chaps out of ten are," Gideon found himself arguing.

"Maybe," said Riddell, "but only while they're on the actual job. There are a lot like me, George, who decided years ago that if we weren't careful, we wouldn't have any home and private life at all. The Yards doesn't *own* us body and soul, you know. That's another angle you might put in this report you're going to draw up. They pay us only about half of what we'd get in a commercial job which needed half the brains, and treat us like a lot of bloody soldiers. At least, they would if we'd let 'em. And if you think you're going to make any impression on the Home Office and the VIPs, you're making the biggest mistake of your life. You'll be in favour while you sweat your guts out for them, and you'll probably get a medal and a pretty speech, but policemen—they're not *people*. Why, they're not even civil servants! Take it from me, Gee-Gee, it's time you stopped banging your head against a brick wall, and just settled down to giving a fair day's work for a fair day's pay. That's all you're paid for and all you owe them."

Gideon's smile had become very set.

"Who are the 'them'?" he asked.

"Our Lords and Masters, who pay us and treat us like puppets. Come under the Home Office, don't we?"

"Hm," said Gideon, and stopped smiling altogether. "Well, you're honest about it, if nothing else."

"But you don't agree with me."

"I think you've got the wrong approach entirely, and I think you're wrong about the number of men who agree with you," argued Gideon, "but that's something else I'm going to find out. I take it you don't like the pressure in this office?"

"It just about drives me up the wall!"

"We can soon stop that," said Gideon. "Get everything on your desk tidied up, with notes about any matters pending, and then go down to Bournsea and help Hill. He needs as much help as he can get."

"No, Gee-Gee——"

"And don't Gee-Gee me!" Gideon roared and was astonished at the harshness of his own voice. "I'm Commander to you in future, and don't you forget it. You blurry fool, if you talked like this in the Army, they'd shoot you."

Riddell said: "Very good, sir," in an icy voice.

Was the problem getting under his skin? Gideon asked himself later in the afternoon, when Riddell had packed his things and gone, and a detective sergeant was at the aide's desk, doing little more than taking and sending out messages. Was he expecting too much not only of Riddell, but all the others? Had he grown so used to extreme pressure on himself that he took it for granted that others ought to feel in the same way? Was he asking more than anyone could possibly expect? Was the best way to get what he wanted, more money for the staff, to allow things to become slack?

Was it really worth fighting?

Scott-Marle had warned him that the best he could reasonably hope for was the *status quo*.

How typical was Riddell of the *status quo*? How far out of touch was he, Gideon, with his men? Were there only a few like Bell, Syd Taylor and Hopkinson?

Hopkinson had said that he could get dozens of volunteers to go down below on the *van Doorn*.

Could he?

"We want someone to go down that gangway," Hopkinson was saying to a group of men not far from the gangway which led to the main deck of the *van Doorn*. "There's a fireman on the way, you'll have fireproof suits if the Slob does get up to his tricks. Single men only."

Seven men said promptly: "I'll go down."

Hopkinson surveyed them and experienced a bad moment, the moment when he knew that he would have to make a decision as to who should go. There was a sound chance that Micky the Slob would be caught without serious trouble, but the ghost of Syd Taylor seemed to be standing by the side of each of these men. Had there been two, he could have said 'toss for it' and got away with that, but now he could not evade the responsibility. One was a detective officer of thirty-odd, a man he knew well, who had no relations and had been widowed for three years; not a daredevil, but an officer who would take considered chances all his life.

"Okay, Forbes," he said.

"Thanks," said Forbes, as if he meant it.

The sun was shimmering on the Thames, where the launches and the small boats kept up their constant patrol. Not far away, ships were being worked, and the whirr of derricks and cranes made a constant background of sound. A fire-fighting trailer had arrived, and Forbes went to join the Chief Officer.

Forbes, who had his fair hair clipped in an American crew-cut, and was a bony man who seldom smiled, was briefed for a few minutes, and then helped into the fireproof suit; he felt as if he was getting ready for deep-sea diving. Then he and the fireman went to the gangway. Movement was surprisingly easy, and he could see the whole scene through the fireproof goggles which covered his eyes. He saw Hopkinson wave, and waved back from the deck of the ship. One dock policeman and a member of the crew were at the top of the hatch leading to the gangway, and the cabin where Micky the Slob was now hiding.

There was a small public address system controlled from the wheelhouse on the bridge, with loudspeakers at various key points. Suddenly Hopkinson's voice came over clearly:

"Micky, we're coming for you if you're not out in five minutes. Don't make things worse than they are."

There was no answer.

"Just drop everything, open the cabin door, and come out," Hopkinson called.

Forbes waited, only two treads behind the fireman.

Up on the bridge of the boat, with the master by his side, Hopkinson could see the whole of the dock area. There was a little confusion at the nearest gate; a woman was there, apparently arguing with the men who were on duty, stopping anyone from coming in or going out. Hopkinson saw this as he saw so many things: almost casually.

"Four minutes," he called, and knew that the warning could be heard in the cabin where the murderer waited; he tried to think of everything he knew about Micky the Slob, to decide whether Micky would really make a fight of it; or try to. If he decided to fight, what would he fight with?

Just the petrol?

Hopkinson saw two men coming at the double, with a woman between them. The sun shone on her dark hair, even on her red lips. She was a dumpy little piece, and as she drew nearer she could see that for her height she had an enormous bosom. She had stumpy little legs, too, and a very pale face. One of the men with her was calling out.

Hopkinson said to a detective sergeant with him:

"Go and see what she wants."

"She answers the description of the girl who tricked Syd Taylor," the sergeant told him.

"That's right. Get going."

The sergeant went hurrying to the side of the deck, and the girl disappeared from sight, hidden by the deck itself. Hopkinson had never been more wary. The sergeant was right about her but he could not think of any way in which she could hope to fool them now. She could fool one man, but not fifty.

The sergeant was shouting.

The girl's voice sounded in reply, but Hopkinson could not hear what she said. All about him the small ships were moving, the men were massed and waiting—and there was that shrill voice warning him.

The sergeant swung round, cupped his hands, and roared:

"She says he's got nitro-glycerine, sir!"

"He has," the girl gasped. She was breathless with running from the dock gates, and the words came out

120

gaspingly. "He said he'd never be caught alive and he'd take as many police as he could with him. He said he'd got petrol for a fire, but he's got nitro."

"Nitro!" roared the sergeant.

Hopkinson clapped a hand over the microphone, and called down clearly:

"Go and get those men back!" He took his hand away from the microphone, and spoke again to Micky the Slob. "Don't let's have trouble for the sake of it, Micky, we'll give you a fair deal. I'll give you another five minutes to think about it."

There was no possibility of an answer; no way of finding out what the trapped man was likely to do. There was not even any certainly that the girl was telling the truth; this might be a kind of trick which Hopkinson had not anticipated.

If she had come to help the Slob, how did she expect to do it?

The sergeant had disappeared down the hatch.

There was no sound.

"Micky," called Hopkinson into the silence, "don't make us come down and get you."

If he had nitro-glycerine, when would he use it?

The girl was climbing from the gangway now, and at closer quarters, Hopkinson saw what a good complexion she had, and her bold good looks; had she not been so dumpy and fat, she would have been remarkably attractive. She was being brought to the bridge.

Then he saw Forbes and the fireman, still in their fireproof clothes, come through from the gangway, and felt a deep sense of relief. The girl—in fact she was thirty or more—came stumbling towards him, still gasping for breath.

"I mean it, he really has got nitro," she told him,

and seemed desperately afraid that he would not believe her. "He really told me he would never be caught alive, and he'd take as many cops as he could with him."

"When did he tell you this?" Hopkinson asked.

"Before he came aboard. I came with him from Pitt Street, see, when he escaped."

"You the girl who trapped Taylor?"

"Yes," she answered tensely; her eyes were bold and bright with fear which Hopkinson could not quite understand; but he found himself believing that she wanted to help the police now. "Yes, I did it, I didn't think they'd kill him! I couldn't sleep all last night thinking about it, that's God's truth. I hoped Micky would get away, but when I heard you'd trapped him here I knew what he'd do, and I couldn't have any more lives on my conscience. For God's sake don't break into that cabin, he'll blow the ship up."

Hopkinson believed her now.

He wondered, gloomily, about the next step. As far as he could tell, they would have to play the game patiently, and hope to wear Micky down, but that would tie up dozens of men for hours, perhaps for days. More: it would be rated as a defeat. The public always sympathised with the man who defied the weight of the law like this, and if they could not get Micky alive, the police would be the laughing stock of every criminal in London.

That wouldn't last for long but it might last long enough to do a great deal of damage.

He thought: "I'd better check with Gideon."

"We want to find a way of getting near enough to that cabin to pump tear gas in," Gideon said.

"It won't do, George."

"Why not?"

"He's only got to drop that nitro, and it'll blow up."

"If our chaps are outside the door, they won't get badly hurt. They'd only get hurt if they had the door open. Try it, Hoppy."

"All right," said Hopkinson, without enthusiasm.

"How many volunteers did you get?" Gideon asked, and could not quite make the question sound casual.

"Seven," answered Hopkinson, and wondered why it mattered. He rang off, turned to the Dutch master, who was in the wheelhouse, and unrolled a plan of the *van Doorn,* on which the barricaded cabin was already marked in red. "What we really need is an engineer who can find a way to get round this way." He traced lines with his fingers.

"Without noise?" The master's voice was very hard. "With noise, he blow up my ship. Without noise, can you do it?"

One man, shutting himself away, could defy a small army of police.

One man, serving behind the counter of a grocer's shop, looking and smiling at three small children who had come in with their mother, was being sought by another army of police.

And in the flat overlooking Hyde Park, Keith Ryman and Rab Stone were arguing about the best way of doing what they set out to do.

10

THE PLOTTERS

Ryman was lying on a luxurious couch, placed in the window overlooking Hyde Park, and his feet were up at one end. Stone sat on the arm of an easy chair, close to him. Both had glasses in their hands; only Stone was smoking. There was uneasiness in his manner, as well as a kind of tension. Ryman was looking out on to the beautiful green of early summer, but from his position could see only the tops of the trees; no building and no people.

"I wouldn't be any use to you if I didn't tell you what I think," Stone said, uncertainly.

Ryman didn't answer.

"It's one thing to fix the coppers," went on Stone, with an obvious effort. "You don't have anything to worry about then, it can't be done in a jiffy. Run over 'em, for instance, or shoot 'em, or——"

"Shut up," Ryman said.

"I'm only giving you the benefit of my advice."

"Shut up."

Stone got up and went to the cocktail cabinet on the other side of the room, poured himself out more whisky, added a splash of soda, and stared at Ryman's eyes, anxiety showing very clearly in his own. The sun was shining on Ryman's feet. He had kicked off his shoes, and showed thin blue socks with a red pattern. The button of his coat was undone, and his tie was a little loose at the neck. He kept swinging his glass round, very slowly. The sound of traffic from Park Lane floated clearly through the window, but it was muted and did not distract.

They were silent for five minutes.

"What I want to make clear is that I'm all for the principle of the thing. I think you're absolutely right about the way snatching a couple of kids would draw the police off, nothing would do it so well," Stone said. "But that's not the only thing to consider, Keith. You may think I'm solid from the neck up, but——"

Ryman looked across at him.

"I do," he said. He swung his feet off the end of the couch and grinned; it was astonishing to see the change in Stone's expression, reflecting the extent of his relief. "You're as solid as a lump of granite, but a little light penetrates at times. Okay, I agree with you, it would be risky to snatch a couple of kids. I'm echoing you, too: they would need hiding out somewhere, someone would have to look after them, you'd need top men to do the job, and if you had top men, you'd need to offer a lot of money. Also, two kids kidnapped on the same day are odorously fishy. So, we stick to cops—mainly."

"I knew you'd see it my way." Stone tossed his drink down. "Want another?"

"No. Two coppers." Ryman went on, dreamily, "and one kid."

Stone stopped, with a hand actually on the neck of the whisky bottle.

"Just one kid," repeated Ryman, and smiled lazily at some fluffy white clouds drifting across the sky.

"Somebody's little angel. Just one will be enough, provided the dear devoted dad is rich enough."

Stone, who had opened his mouth to speak, did not say a word, but a new expression showed in his eyes.

"Interest you?" asked Ryman, in the same smooth voice. "I thought it would. What you have to do is *think*, Rabby, my boy, it's no use jumping your fences. We want some honest to goodness distractions, but there's no reason why we shouldn't make a good thing out of one of them. No one could ever make a good thing out of a copper, but a child with a millionaire father and loving momma—how about that?"

Stone said slowly: "It's a new angle, anyway."

"It's as old as any angle in the game, the new thing will be the motive behind it. Heads we win, tails they lose! If we can pick up a large piece of money for the little angel, that will be fine, but the main job will still be the appropriating of a certain large sum of used banknotes, the only kind of boodle that it's really safe to use *and* store away. We happen to know that the Mid-London Bank in Leadenhall Street has a large sum of ready available from time to time, and we have a contact who will tell us the right day to raid it. The boodle will be loaded into a armoured car. We shall have the driver of the armoured car on our side. Don't interrupt, and don't tell me it's an old trick, there's nothing new under the sun." He glanced across at Stone. "If I'm repeating myself, don't stop me. Beneath this brilliant flow of badinage there is an astute mind ticking away like a calculating machine. The end of the month is the best time for Mid-London, according to my information, and that should suit us nicely. It's the tenth today. How long will it take you to get two coppers lined up?"

"I can do it this week," Stone said.

"Get information about the two most likely to suit

126

our purpose," ordered Ryman. "We want two coppers whom someone hates enough to kill. Let me know by the end of the week certain, and I'll tackle my Mid-London Bank friend. How about that, Rabbie, old boy? Sound better?"

"Which kid are you going to snatch?" asked Stone, obviously still uneasy.

"I shall make a survey of the field, and advise you in due course," Ryman promised him airily. "Have no fears, it shall be done."

"Keith——"

"Now cut out the arguing," said Ryman, sharply. "You've got to lay on the men for those coppers and you've got to get a good driver ready for the banknote snatch. I'll go into that, too. Better lay on two drivers, we'll want to switch cars as soon as we can. That's the important thing about a bank-van snatch, to leave the van stranded as soon as you can. You're a practical man, so you work out what we'll need in addition to two fast drivers. Allow for enough men to empty that van in five minutes, too. Got it?"

"Yes."

"And leave the snatch and the worrying to me," said Ryman. "I shan't leave it to you, believe me! I'll handle the snatch myself, because I won't want anybody with unsteady nerves to be involved. I'll fix that, then, you get plans out for the rest."

"Okay, Keith."

"And look happy about it!"

"Keith," said Stone, with a stubbornness which did not come easily, "I'm still not happy about snatching children, I just don't like it. But you know the risks, so okay. Will Helen be in this?"

"You bet Helen will be in this," replied Ryman, softly. "She wouldn't be sentimental, like some people

127

I know; didn't I tell you that her heart was made of diamonds!"

"Well, it's up to you," Stone conceded. "Got any preference about the policemen? Are they to be plain-clothes yobs or uniformed men?"

"Don't see that it matters," said Ryman, and grinned suddenly. "Why not one of each? All you have to make sure is that someone hates them enough to put them away with a bit of prompting. Should be easy enough, shouldn't it?"

"It'll be easy," Stone assured him. "In fact I think I could name them this very minute. I was talking with Si last night."

"Who are they?" Ryman asked sharply.

"A flatfoot named Maybell——"

"What's that?"

Stone grinned.

"You heard me—Maybell, Horace Maybell. He's a Sergeant at Hammersmith, been there for donkey's years. He put Charlie Daw away for ten years—if it hadn't been for Maybell, Daw would have got away with it. Copped him climbing out of a window. Daw always said he'd get Maybell the minute he came out, and he was released a month ago. Stony broke, too. For a couple of hundred nicker he'd slit anyone's throat. It needs laying on carefully, but Si'll see to that. Couple of hundred okay to promise?"

"Yes, but don't specify who the victim's to be, yet. Next?"

"Don't tell me you've got a bad memory," Stone said, half sneering. "You haven't forgotten Arch the *He*-ro. He's the brand new detective officer out at NE Division—just been transferred from uniform to plain-clothes because of the great courage he showed in stopping a smash and grab car from running away. Jumped on the running-board, and had a fight with the driver——"

"Until it crashed, and the driver was killed, a chap named Cartwright. That the job?"

"That's the job. Cartwright's father didn't say a word at the inquest, but Si told me he's looking for a chance to even things out."

"They both sound right," Ryman agreed, thoughtfully. "Just get me more details and talk to Si about it, but don't make any approach to these chaps yet, I might get a better idea." There was a hard glint in his clear blue eyes as he stared across the park; he was now sitting up on the couch. "Give it all plenty of time to soak."

"Okay, Keith."

"And don't worry," Ryman added. "I must know two or three millionaires who'd gladly pay a few thousand for their angelic offspring, and when the kid's missing, there'll be the biggest hunt ever. We won't mention ransom until we've pulled the bank job, either. It's a certain winner."

Stone said: "Sure," and finished his drink and went out.

Ryman settled down on the couch, wriggled himself comfortable, folded his hands across his chest, closed his eyes, and appeared to doze.

Police Sergeant Maybell was cycling round his district in Hammersmith, stopping to talk to every constable on the beat, whether green or experienced, and also talking to the traffic-duty men. He led a somewhat prosaic existence, and enjoyed it. He had a plumply comfortable wife and three children, two boys in their late teens and a girl aged eleven. He was fifty-nine, and did not intend to retire until he was sixty-five, when he would have to. He was a thorough-going and conscientious officer, who seldom recalled the fact that many years ago he had been instrumental in catching a burglar, named Daw, who had been sentenced to ten years' imprisonment for robbery with violence.

Nothing really sensational had affected Maybell's life since then.

Detective Officer David Archer, at twenty-seven, was one of the seven policemen who had stepped forward to volunteer for the attempt to get Micky the Slob out of the *van Doorn*. Archer had a great deal in his favour. He was good-looking, he had done well in a grammar school, spent two years at London University, and then decided that he wanted a career in the Metropolitan Police, because he thought it would give him more scope than an ordinary civilian job. He was extremely ambitious, without offending anyone by it, and without having the slightest desire to tread on anyone's else's toes in order to get ahead. Six months ago he had taken the chance to stop the smash and grab raider's car and knew that as a consequence he had been put into the detective branch much earlier than he would normally have hoped.

Recently, he had acquired an even greater reason for being ambitious.

He had become engaged to be married.

He was at the dockside, near the *van Doorn*, feeling a little superfluous like most of the men now kicking their heels at Micky the Slob's bidding, when Gideon stepped out of a big black car; the sight of Gideon's bulk and the way he swung his arms as he strode towards Hopkinson, the girl and a little group of Divisional men, sent a kind of electric shock through every watcher.

Archer had a strange impression: that everyone near him wanted to raise a cheer.

Gideon had the same feeling, and it took him completely by surprise. It was some time since he had been among any of the Divisional police when they were in strength. He knew that he was something of a legend in the Force, that every one of the twenty thousand men on it knew that Gee-Gee was George Gideon's nickname, and that there was a kind of rude affection in their use of it; as there was for Hippo Hill's nickname. But it was only occasionally that Gideon had a sense of real enthusiasm passing itself on from the men to him. They had read the Sunday newspapers, of course, and were all solidly behind him; had this been a different occasion, they would probably have given a spontaneous cheer.

Hopkinson came forward, leaving the girl behind him. He saw Gideon studying the girl, and said as he drew up:

"That's her, George, if we could stretch her out to normal height, she'd be quite something. But what's brought you?"

"Had an idea," said Gideon.

"You're changing!"

Gideon hardly noticed the words, and continued to look at the girl, with her dark hair, her fine colouring, her bright, bold eyes. She was aware of his scrutiny, and did nothing to try to avoid it.

"Let's have it," Hopkinson urged.

"Right," said Gideon, and looked away from the girl. "She's got a conscience, or she wouldn't have come. You say she said she couldn't sleep last night, because Taylor had died, and because she was afraid of what Slob would do."

131

"That's right." Hopkinson didn't yet understand.

"She in love with him?"

"Incredible though it may seem, yes."

"He with her?"

Hopkinson was frowning, and the bright sunlight, pitiless on his face, showed up every tiny line and every grey hair.

"That's how the story goes."

"What about his wife?"

"He keeps her, doesn't he? But I don't see what you're driving at," the Divisional man said.

"The girl did a lot for Micky the Slob," Gideon said, "and now she knows that he's had it. She's got guts and a conscience, too. Think she could reason with Micky?" Gideon kept watching her. "Think we could persuade her to go down and plead with him?"

"It wouldn't work, George," Hopkinson declared, and his expression added: "You must be slipping or you wouldn't even suggest it."

"That's right, it wouldn't work," Gideon agreed. "But if he's really fond of her, and thought she was actually outside the door while our chaps were breaking it down, would he use the nitro? That would mean blowing her to smithereens, as well as our chaps."

"God!" exclaimed Hopkinson. "That's an idea. But who——"

"This is a job we can't delegate to anyone," Gideon said. "That's why I came out. Mind if I talk to the girl?"

"You carry on!"

"Name of Rose, didn't you say?" asked Gideon, and went towards the girl, towering high above her head. He smiled as he stood in front of her, and spoke very quietly. "I want to tell you how grateful everyone is for your courage," he said deliberately. "Not only the police, but the crew of the ship are, too. Are you also willing to help us get Micky out before he can do any more harm?"

She hesitated for along time. Then:

"How?" she asked.

11

CAPTURE

Inside the cabin, Micky the Slob was reclining on a
bunk, his head bent so that he did not touch the bunk
above him. It was a large cabin for a small ship, and
there were four bunks with plenty of space to move
around. Men's clothes were draped on hangers in several places. Four sets of shaving-brushes, tooth brushes,
tubes of tooth paste and of shaving-cream crowded the
big shelf on the one dressing-table. On a chair by the
side of Micky the Slob was a large slab of plain chocolate and some packets of biscuits; on the floor two
bottles of beer and an empty glass. He kept his porcine
eyes half closed, but stared at the door all the time.

Sticking in the neck of an empty beer bottle was a
cigar-shaped container, and inside this, looking like a
fat cigarette, was a tube of nitro-glycerine. The experts
at blowing doors and safes had perfected a way of carrying explosive, and for a price it was possible to buy
a stick like this. It was enough to blow open three or
four powerful safes or strong-room doors; enough to
wreck this cabin and start a fire which would destroy
the ship.

The explosive, in its container, looked like a kind of candle

A crackling came from the loud-speaker, built into the ceiling; Micky glanced upwards, but saw only the crisscross lines of the steel lattice work of the bunk above him. There was a sound, as of someone blowing, and then a different voice from Hopkinson's. Micky sat up, opened his eyes wide, and bent his head so that he could look up at the loudspeaker.

"Glad you've been sensible so far, Micky," the new-comer said, and there was a deep, authoritative note in his voice. "We've got someone here to help you to see the wise thing to do. Rose Lemman's on her way down the gangway to see you. We've pulled her in."

Micky was still sitting, crouching, head twisted so that he could see the loudspeaker. It was never possible to be sure what he was thinking, and his expression seldom changed; but now his lips were set tightly, and there was no sign of a slobber.

"She did the best thing she could for you," the man with the deep hard voice went on. "Don't let her down. She'll be just outside your door by now."

Micky eased himself forward and got off the bunk. His leg was within an inch of the beer bottle with its high-explosive 'candle'. One kick, and it would fall over, out of its safety packing; the concussion would be enough to make it explode.

"And she knows what's good for herself, too," Gideon went on. "She knows that if you do any more harm, we'll have to charge her with being an accessory to Taylor's murder. She'll be the only one left we can get for that job, and she helped all right. But if she persuades you not to blow this ship to pieces, we shall be able to make things a bit easier for her. You could help us. She says she didn't know you were going to murder Taylor, and you're the only one who can say whether

135

she did or not. We *want* to believe her," the speaker added, and broke off abruptly.

Micky muttered: "That's Gideon."

A little frothy saliva was gathering at the corners of his mouth, and his lower lip began to drop, as if he could not support it any longer. He looked like an imbecile as he stared at the silent loudspeaker, licked his lips again, and glanced down, as if unthinking, at the 'candle'.

He bent down and picked it up.

Gideon said: "You're the only chance she's got, Micky. Give her a break."

Micky was breathing noisily through his mouth. His big hand was tight about the beer bottle, but he still stared at the ceiling. Then came Rose's voice, very distantly, and the direction of Micky's gaze changed swiftly; he watched the door.

She must be just outside.

"Micky," she called, "it's no use trying any more, it won't do any good, honestly."

He didn't answer.

"Micky," she called again, and he could tell that she was much nearer; there was a break in her voice. "It's all UP, don't you understand? I did my best, but they got me. They'll make me swing; they hang you for killing a copper even today."

Again she stopped.

Micky the Slob held the bottle even more tightly, raised it, and yet continued to stare at the closed door. He heard nothing for what seemed a long time, and then the voice of Gideon came through the doorway; so he had left the bridge house and was just outside.

"All right, Rose," he said. "You've done your best. Just stand over there."

Rose gasped: *"Micky!"*

"He won't let you down," Gideon said. "I'm sure of

136

that. Micky, be careful with that nitro-glycerine, it's nasty stuff to handle. We're coming in now. Just move aside, Rose, you're in the way.

"Micky, don't blow us up!" Rose pleaded; and then there came three smashing blows on the wooden door, the steel of an axe glinted, disappeared, glinted twice again; then a gaping hole appeared in the wood, and a man was visible behind it. This man thrust his hand through the hole and groped for the key on the lock. He touched it. He was all Micky could see, just a big hand, thumb and forefinger on the key now; turning. The bottle seemed to be slipping from Micky's fingers. Saliva dropped.

"Keep back, Rose!" Gideon said sharply. "I don't want you——"

He drew his hand back through the hole, and a moment later the door swung open. Micky did not even move, and Gideon, with two men just behind him, stretched out his hand and took the bottle; he did not wrench at it, or show any violence, just drew it away easily.

He said in a strange, quiet voice: "Okay, Micky, don't let's have any fuss, and we'll do all we can for your Rose."

Micky the Slob did not speak. A man behind Gideon, tall, young, good-looking, slipped handcuffs on the prisoner, chaining him to his own wrist. Other men came hurrying. There was no sign of Rose Lemman outside the cabin, but she was at the top, staring down at him, crying.

When Micky reached the top of the companion-way, with men all round him, he looked at Rose's eyes, and said:

"You don't have to worry, they'll see you right. Won't you, Gideon?"

"We'll see her right," Gideon said.

Micky the Slob *smiled.*

When he had gone, when the crew were coming back on board, and when the police were questioning the master and others about the fact that the Slob had hidden here, Gideon was driving back to Scotland Yard. He felt rather tired, but very satisfied. By his side was the small tape recorder, on which Rose had recorded everything that Micky the Slob had heard her say. Young Archer, of the NE Division, had suggested it.

The ruse had worked, and that was the only thing that mattered.

When Gideon got back to his office, the first thing he asked the middle-aged sergeant on duty was:

"Anything from Bournsea?"

"Not a word."

"Thought we might have two strokes of luck at the same time."

"If you can call it luck," the sergeant said. "Certainly lucky you weren't blown to smithereens, sir. It *was* nitro, wasn't it?"

"It looked like nitro, it was packed like nitro, and it terrified me the same as nitro would," said Gideon. "It's upstairs in the lab, being tested. If you hear an explosion, you'll know it was the real stuff. Anything in?"

"They got the killer at Scarborough."

Gideon's eyes lit up.

"The child killer?"

"Yes."

"Who?"

"The father."

"Oh, God," breathed Gideon.

"What people do," the sergeant said, flatly. "They picked up Sammy Lees for the fur job the other night, forget when it was. A1 Division reports a six-year-old child missing, and they want half the blooming Force to go and help them; you've only got to mention a missing child and they blow. Nasty job out at Portobello Road, knife fight. A white man and a Jamaican are in hospital; the blackie might die. The white chap started it, out of jealousy. Picked up Teddy the Loop over in CD. Copped him with the sparklers lifted from Samson's of Piccadilly the other day, so they've started a search of his house. Looks as if he's got plenty tucked away under the floorboards. Couple of small holdups, one in Putney, one in Tottenham. I don't know how you like it done but I've scrawled everything down, date, time and all details as far as I know. Need four cars and four pairs of hands on this job."

Gideon was looking at him very straightly.

"How long have you been here, Jim?"

"Five years longer than you, George!"

Gideon began to smile.

"You've done me a world of good," he said. "Thanks. Chief Inspector Bell will be moving in here for a while, and you'll have to nurse him. You've got the right approach to this job."

The other man's eyes showed real alarm, and he raised his right hand to his almost bald head.

"You *leaving?* Oh, I get it, you've been made Assistant Commissioner! Well, no one ever deserved——"

"Take it easy," Gideon said. "I'm not likely to get an AC's job, whether I want it or not. I'm going to concentrate on building up a case to convince the Home Office and the Treasury that we need half a million quid, and that'll keep me busy for a while."

"Always did believe in miracles, didn't you?" the sergeant said.

Gideon grinned.

* * *

He looked up, a little after six o'clock, and was surprised to see Rogerson coming in. The Assistant Commissioner had two evening newspapers in his hand, and he was smiling dryly as he asked:

"Seen these, George?"

"No. What's in 'em?"

"Glutton for publicity, that's your trouble." Rogerson gibed. And there was Gideon looking up at himself again from each front page. There was young Archer, too, and of course Rose Lemman. "No one who knows you is surprised, but if you stick your neck out again while I'm in charge of this department, I'll reprimand you in public." Rogerson's smile had an edge to it. "And I'm not resigning, I'm applying for six months' sick leave instead. You'll have to do your own job and mine from now until Christmas."

Gideon took a chance.

"Carrying on as usual," he said.

Rogerson chuckled.

George Arthur Smith read the evening newspaper, and all about the search for himself.

Micky the Slob was allowed to see one paper, in the cell at Cannon Row.

Sergeant Maybell read the front page just before going off duty.

"That Gideon must have joined the Force the same month as I did," he confided to a sergeant who was taking over for the night. "Never looked back, he hasn't."

Dave Archer read the story while with his fiancée, who was very pleasant to look at, who dressed well,

140

and who knew exactly what she wanted. Just then she was a little scared.

"Don't be too much of a hero, Dave, will you?" she asked.

All the Gideon family read it, and Kate's anxiety was almost overshadowed by the great pride of the children.

Millions of people read the story . . .

Keith Ryman was one of them, and he stood staring at the photograph of Gideon, while his Helen, in bra and panties, peered at the reflection of her pretty, pert face in the mirror.

"Now there's a man to get," Ryman muttered. "That would draw them off all right."

"Say something, pet?" called Helen.

"Nothing that matters," Ryman called back, still staring at the photograph.

Gideon went to the Yard next morning with only one real regret in his mind: that the Bournsea job was going cold on him. He had already talked to Hill, by telephone, and Hill had reported another night without any results at all.

"We've talked to ninety-eight per cent of the licensed dog owners," he had said. "There's always the odd few who don't take out a licence, but they're going to be much more difficult to get at. There's been plenty of time for the swine to kill his dog, of course, so we're well on the way to checking dogs which have disappeared. At least we've a fairly good description."

"Something will turn up," Gideon said, unhelpfully.

"I hope to God we don't get another kid murdered." Hill could not have sounded more concerned if he had been talking of his own children. "You're keeping your end up, anyhow, but don't go and get yourself hurt, we need you for a bit longer."

"You'd forget me inside a week," Gideon said.

But the remark cheered him up very much.

The first job he did at the Yard was to study all the circumstances of the Bournsea murders, hoping to discern some factor which had been missed, but he saw none. It looked like a model operation of its kind, with the Yard and the County Borough and the County Police all dovetailing well. Twenty thousand inquiries had been made in three days. The peak had been passed, of course; men wanted for their normal duties would go back to them today. At least Hill was as good a man as they had for it.

He hadn't mentioned Riddell.

The sergeant had prepared all the reports and had them on his desk as efficiently as Gideon's absent chief assistant could have done.

"I'll have him here with Bell," Gideon decided, and his thoughts were lured off the problems in front of him for several minutes, while he contemplated the difficulties in presenting the case for the Home Secretary. It was an unpalatable fact that the pressure of the two main inquiries, at Bournsea and at the London Docks, had made it impossible for him to do more than skim the surface of the 'case'. Even now, he had to put consideration of it aside, and call in the officers dealing with the diverse cases on his desk.

He got through this quickly.

"I'll spend the afternoon drawing up a kind of brief," he consoled himself, and forgot the 'case' as he thought again of Bournsea.

* * *

It was a beautiful afternoon at Bournsea, and there was no outward sign of alarm on the beaches. Yet parents kept a closer watch on their children and every dog, from peke to labrador, was watched warily. In the hot back streets of the town, police and detectives worked patiently. Hill had a brainwave, and consulted the post office and the main delivery trades, the milk and the bread. All postmen and roundsmen were asked to take special note of any dog answering the description of the handsome mongrel, and particularly to report if any such dog appeared to be missing. As postmen did a daily coverage, they might produce a quick result.

George Arthur Smith looked cool and neat in his short white jacket as he served the customers who drifted in. The afternoon was never a busy period for the grocer's shop, and he had plenty of time to look out of the window and the doorway. The small shop served a neighbourhood where there were many young families in small new houses, and he saw the children as they passed on their way home from school.

It was a little after four o'clock.

Two or three children always came in, for a small bar of chocolate, a few sweets, a packet of chewing gum; and some of the older boys came to try to buy some cigarettes. All of these goods were kept handy, near the doorway, and Smith watched the children approaching. Here, they took different roads, and most of them looked each way, most carefully. A small group of boys and girls, all very young, reached the shop and stood looking in at the window.

Smith saw one girl with fair hair tied in a bright pink ribbon, her face aglow with eagerness, her eyes cornflower blue. By comparison, the other children were pale and uninteresting. Smith watched this eager child, saw her forefinger stubbed against the window, and be-

143

gan to gulp; he could never understand the effect that golden-haired children had over him. Most children left him cold, but any girl with golden hair made his blood race. He wanted to be alone with them, to hold and caress them, to make them still and silent. He did not consciously remember the neighbour's child and his own 'sweetheart', only knew that his heart beat so fast that it seemed as if he would suffocate. And whenever a girl was still and silent, he had a terrible headache.

All three children moved quickly, and came into the shop, the fair-haired one showing a sixpence in her hot palm.

Smith moistened his lips; and then smiled.

"Hullo, and how are you?"

She looked straight at the sweets counter, pointed, and said:

"I want one of those and one of those."

"Little girls should say please," chided Smith.

"Please."

He selected the wrapped sweets and handed them to her one at a time; each time his fingers slid over her chubby little hand, lingeringly; she did not seem to notice. She handed him the sixpence. He hesitated, then decided it would not be wise to refuse, so he squeezed her hand tightly, took the coin and said:

"Come and see me again, soon."

She stared at him as if he puzzled her, and then danced out, with the others waiting to share the sweets. Smith wiped his forehead and stood very still. He watched the sun shining on that fair hair as, dipping into one of the bags, the child passed the window.

He went to the door and looked along at her until she turned the corner.

A postman on his way home cycled past, nodded to him, but did not look back. Smith went into the shop, and then into the little back parlour. His mother was in the garden, pulling up a few weeds, and he saw her standing still for a moment, looking at the kennel. Soon afterwards she came in, and her first words were:

"It's a funny thing that dog hasn't come back, I've never known him away for so long before."

"I'm worried in case he's met with an accident." Smith said, glibly. "He was always difficult crossing the road."

"Well, it's a funny thing," his mother repeated.

Smith stared at her.

She looked up at him with rather watery eyes, which did not serve her well, and he could not be sure what she was thinking about; certainly she stared at him much longer than she usually did. She could not read the newspapers, and he usually read her the headlines, and any spicy paragraphs; but she listened regularly to the news broadcasts.

Had she heard about the search for a dog?

If she had——

She said: "Well, if you're going down for your dip today, you'd better get off, Georgie, I'll look after the shop until you're back."

He hated her calling him 'Georgie'.

"Thanks, Mum." He had already decided that he must not go to the beach for along time, in case anyone recognised him: but he did not want to say so, for he had made a habit of a daily swim for years. "I'll get my towel and trunks." He went upstairs in the little house, came down with the roll of swimming clothes, went to the garden and stuffed them in his saddle-bag, then cycled off. The sight of his dog trotting alongside him on the cycle as quite common in the neighbourhood; the kind of sight that people saw so often that it was hardly noticed.

He cycled along a street of small new bungalows and

bright new gardens. Just in front of one house a group of children were playing, among them the fair-haired child.

She did not notice him.

He wondered if she lived at this house, and noted the number: 51.

He cycled on, but kept away from the beach, although he missed the gaiety and the life, the splashing water and the children who were forever playing. He could not rid his mind of the fact that the police were swarming over the beach, and questioning everybody. He kept thinking of the detective who had questioned him, and the fact that he had given a false name and address.

He was frightened.

Later, when he had gone out to the pictures, his mother found the towel and the swimming-trunks, all quite dry. She felt the clothes with her skinny fingers, time and time again. Then she went out and looked at the kennel, where their dog had been for several weeks, since they had bought him. She had prayed that the company of a dog would help George, who seemed so lonely and was undoubtedly a little peculiar.

When they had first had the dog, they had not been sure whether to keep it, so they had not taken out a licence. That didn't matter now, but she was remembering a conversation she had had, late on Sunday evening, with the wife of a local police constable. It had been about the murdered children.

The police were looking for a man who often went swimming at the beach, with his dog.

"Georgie," Mrs Smith said, in a hoarse voice: "Oh, Georgie."

And soon:

"What shall I do?"

"It can't be him, it can't be!"

That evening, Dave Archer was much more intent on watching his Drusilla as she prepared to serve, than on returning her service. She looked good, although in fact she was not beautiful. He preferred women who were tall and slim to the buxom kind. She had long, beautiful legs, no one could deny that.

She aced him.

"Game and set," he called, and went to meet her at the net. "Jolly good game you played."

"You weren't concentrating; I think you were thinking about that man Gideon."

Archer burst out laughing.

"Didn't enter my head," he said, "but a little later I'll tell you what I was thinking about." He slid his arm round her waist, and squeezed.

"Careful," she said hastily. "Everyone's staring at us."

"Let 'em stare," said Archer, and he looked gay, handsome and strong. "Let's give 'em something to stare at, too." He swung her round and kissed her; she was laughing when he let her go.

"Bert," said Mrs Maybell, "there's something I've been meaning to ask you for some time."

"Is there, dear? What's that?"

"Do you think you could avoid night duty, in future?"

"Well, I could put in an application," said Maybell, "but I don't think I'd have much luck. Not worried at being at home alone at night, are you, after all these years?"

147

"I'm not worried about me," his wife said. She was a pleasant, plump, grey-haired woman, with rosy cheeks, a small nose, and calm eyes. They were alone in their bedroom, getting ready for bed. "I'm worried about you, I don't think it's good for you to be on nights so often."

"Been doing my share for thirty-one years," Maybell reminded her.

"Well, it's time someone else did it, for a change."

Her husband grinned at her, and gave her a quick, almost impersonal hug.

"Wanting a bit more company in bed, that's your trouble," he said. "I can't say I'm not with you, but joking apart, Liz, I'd never get off nights, couldn't do the job properly if I didn't take my turn. Don't you worry about me, I'm good for another twenty years, most of it with a pension. When I'm home all day you'll wish to goodness you could shove me back on to the beat."

"If I haven't seen too much of you in thirty years, I don't see why I should see too much in the future," his wife said. "Oh, don't be daft!" She slapped his hand away from the V of her nightdress.

But she was smiling.

12

GIDEON PREPARES

Bell was one of the few men at the Yard who would not need briefing to stand-in for Gideon. On the Tuesday morning he was at the office at eight-thirty, and so was Culverson, the grey-haired sergeant. When Gideon arrived, just before nine, they had the morning reports in perfect order, and a few notes added for Gideon's especial interest. It had been a quiet night, and a goodish day the day before. Gideon looked through the reports, made one or two comments, and then said to Bell:

"You'll see all the chaps, Joe."

"Yes. What shall I tell them you're doing? Having another photograph taken?"

"Tell 'em that I'm preparing the case for the prosecution," Gideon said, and smiled grimly. "The AC is taking some sick leave, so I'm going to use his office. I won't be far away. Let me know if there's anything fresh on the Bournsea job, won't you?"

"We won't keep anything big away from you," Bell promised.

Gideon went along to Rogerson's office, a larger one than his own, with a single big desk. It was a better-than-average room, with a thick piled carpet, a few filing cabinets and some easy chairs; a kind of conference-room-cum-lounge. He went to the window and looked out on the same pleasant river view that he had from his own office, and then opened the door which led to a smaller room, where Rogerson's secretary was sitting at a typewriter.

She was fifty, birdlike, brisk.

"Good morning, Commander. Would you like me to come in now?"

"Soon," said Gideon. "You know what we're going to concentrate on, don't you?"

"Yes, and not before it's time," she said.

So even Miss Sharp approved.

Gideon went back to the desk, loosened his collar and tie, took out his big pipe and stuck it, unlit, between his teeth. He began to write, in a slow and deliberate hand, making a list which began:

1. The Yard.
2. The Divisions. Make out separate sheet for each Division.
3. Make out separate sheet for each department at the Yard, Fingerprints, Records, Photographs, Ballistics, Laboratory, etc. etc.
4. Talk to each department head and each Divisional Superintendent, telling them exactly what I want.
5. Get angle from Popple and the Solicitor's office. [Ask the OM if I can have Keen.]
6. See other Commanders, and get their angle.

He put this sheet aside, after studying it, and then without haste started working on another heading it:

Details Required

1. Actual number of staff now attached.
2. Break this down into [a] CID, [b] Uniformed, [c] Civilian.
3. Get comparative figures, year by year, since 1939.
4. Get statistics of crimes in each Division and break down to [a] indictable and [b] non-indictable.
5. Prepare graphs for each Division and the Yard, comparing [a] crime statistics and [b] staff figures.
6. Prepare a comparative graph for the whole of the Department

    Purpose of all this, to show how crimes increased and staff decreased. Necessary to bring in the uniformed figures—better butter up the U chaps a bit, need many more men on the beat, etc.

He studied this for ten minutes or more, altering a word here, and a word there. He could just hear the typewriter going in the next office; Miss Sharp was clearing up everything that Rogerson had left her to do. There had been no single telephone call in half an hour, no opening door, none of the continual rush and tear of his own office. He wondered how Bell and the sergeant were getting on; damned funny about Culverson, he had been wasting his time doing odds and ends, little more than a messenger because of his sprained ankle, and he could make a real job of assistant to the Commander. He was too old for promotion, that was the trouble; unless he, Gideon, could persuade the next conference that an exception should be made. Or why not suggest that Culverson be transferred from the CID to the civilian branch, and turned into a secretary? That way he could get a couple of hundred a year more, and a better pension.

Gideon turned back to his list, and started a new

one, after marking the others 'A' and 'B'. He headed the one marked 'C':

CID Only
Yard and Divisions

1. Request from each Division and department details of overtime worked.
2. Ditto, holidays outstanding.
3. Average hours worked per man, per week.
4. Number of cases where shortage of staff specifically impedes necessary action. NB. These cases must each be substantiated by details, *eg* the Taylor case.
5. Estimated number of active CID men from Detective Officers upwards needed to give absolute coverage. [Break this down by rank.]
6. Office space, etc. Additional space required.
7. Age of buildings, floor space available, etc. etc.

Gideon put his pencil down, took his pipe out of his mouth, and said with a one-sided grin: "I'm getting tired, or I wouldn't write crap like that." He read through each of the sheets again, then pulled a fourth towards him, headed it 'D' and wrote

In addition to lists A, B, and C, get confidential reports from all senior officers on the quality of their staff and on members of the staff ill, or less than 100% effective because of overwork.
Get reports on general attitude of all staff, *eg* Riddell.
Find comparative incomes for different grades in the following:
   Armed services
   Post Office
   Civil Service

152

Industry

Commerce

in endeavor to show that men are making positive sacrifice at the moment.

Suggest rates of pay needed to stimulate [a] men already on the Force and [b] recruitment.

He put this aside, glanced at his watch, and was surprised to find that it was half past eleven. He got up and stretched, trying to remember the last occasion when an hour and a half had passed without a single interruption; it seldom happened. But he was beginning to miss the constant flow of news.

There was a tap at the communicating door.

"Come in."

Miss Sharp appeared.

"The Assistant Commissioner usually has a cup of tea or coffee at eleven-fifteen, Commander. Would you like to make that a general rule, too?"

Gideon rubbed his chin.

"Good idea," he said. "Do we get that stuff from the canteen?"

"I make it myself, sir."

"Fine, I don't mind which. White coffee with a little sugar, or tea without sugar but a little milk."

"I shall bring you a pot, sir, and the milk and sugar separately," said Miss Sharp, in a tone of mild reproof. "I'm afraid it will be a little late this morning." She went out, closing the door silently behind her. Gideon was grinning at it when the telephone bell rang, startlingly loud in the otherwise silent room. He strode to the desk and lifted the receiver.

"This is the Commissioner's secretary speaking, sir," said a woman briskly. "There will be a brief meeting of Assistant Commissioners—not of departmental heads—this afternoon at four o'clock, and Sir Reginald hopes you will be free to attend."

Gideon said: "I'll be there, unless something unexpected turns up."

"Thank you, sir."

As he rang off, Gideon raised his eyebrows, and soberly considered what he had just said: that something might crop up to prevent him from doing the Commissioner's bidding. There were perks in the AC's job, but he had never been sure that it would really attract him. The next six months would show, and meanwhile it was time he was very careful of what he said to the Commissioner.

Then Miss Sharp came in with a small tray, a spotless white cloth on it, a china coffee pot, hot milk, brown sugar crystals, and some wholemeal biscuits.

Gideon spent an hour in his own office before going to the conference; Bell and Culverson had everything under control. Only one serious job had come in: a request from Norfolk for help to investigate a haystack fires mystery, in which a man had been burned to death.

"Who've we got to send?" asked Gideon.

"Mickle got back from France this morning. He's done all he can on that forged franc job, says that the Frenchies aren't much farther ahead with it," answered Bell. "I wanted to give him a couple of days off."

"What about Bert Challis?"

"He'd be about as much use in the country as a barrow boy!"

"I dunno," Gideon said. "Try him, Joe."

"Right," said Bell.

"If I'm wanted, I'm with the Old Man."

Gideon walked off to the conference, decided that he would have to study the lists he had prepared, draw them up into a kind of schedule of memoranda, and then distribute copies to anyone who was going to help. He ought to have at least ten copies. It wouldn't be a bad idea to take his rough notes home tonight and let Kate have a look at them. He reached the Commissioner's office two minutes ahead of time and found the other AC's and the Deputy Commissioner already there. He was chaffed by two of these and solemnly congratulated on the dockside job by two others, and then sat down to a discussion on a subject he seldom thought about: road accidents.

The latest monthly figures were in, and were on the whole five per cent worse than the corresponding month of the previous year; the figures were undoubtedly worsening all the time. It was not specifically a matter for the Metropolitan Police, but for years the Traffic and Uniformed branches had studied the problem and made recommendations, few of which had been carried out. Gideon made no comment at all during the meeting, but answered one or two specific questions and, when he was on his way back to his office, found himself forced to consider the accident rate and compare it with the indictable crime rate. It was alarming. Nearly six hundred deaths and seventeen thousand serious injuries in one *month*. Compare those figures with the deaths by murder; twenty-seven in the month. Even allowing for the difference in intent, this was an illuminating disproportion: killed with intent, twenty-seven; killed by accident or carelessness five-hundred and seventy-four.

It was easy to understand a man like Prendergast, the Assistant Commissioner for Traffic, thinking that he really had a man-size problem.

Gideon had a very thoughtful, rather uneasy half an hour afterwards. It was undoubtedly true that he had been so obsessed by his own department and its problems that he had not thought seriously enough about the others. The danger now might be that he would widen his perspective at the expense of his effectiveness with the CID.

"Not if I know it," he said to himself, and entered the AC's office. His desk was very tidy, obviously Miss Sharp had been in here, and there was a note: "Can you call Mr. Bell?" and several memos from the various departments; but there was no sign of his pencilled notes. He dived for the waste-paper basket: they weren't there. He strode to the door; if that damned woman had destroyed those papers in an excess of orderliness, he'd just about let her know it.

She was typing very fast; one of those typists whose fingers moved but whose hands seemed only to hover over the keys. She glanced up, eyes bright and alert behind pincenez.

"I left some notes on my desk," Gideon said, peremptorily.

"Yes, Commander, and I knew you would not need them for at least an hour so I typed them in triplicate. I thought you might find that helpful.

Gideon felt completely deflated; and as he looked down at the woman, was sure that her eyes were twinkling behind those lenses; she was not the sobersides she appeared to be. She had straight, greying hair drawn back from her forehead with a comb and tied at the back with a black ribbon; it gave her a slightly Grecian look, with her white shirt blouse and grey skirt.

"That's fine," he said, at last. "Thanks. Do you believe in working overtime?"

"Whenever it's necessary, of course, but the Assistant Commissioner always arranged not to keep me late on Wednesday, when I go to my art classes."

"Art classes," Gideon echoed, and rubbed his chin in a way which had become a habit which he did not know about. "I'll remember that. I thought you might like to take a copy of these notes home, study them, and let me know what you think about them in the morning. What I want is the angle of people who aren't so prejudiced as I am."

"I'll gladly do *that*," Miss Sharp agreed. "In fact, I'd like to, sir, but I think I'm just as prejudiced as you."

On his way home, in a better humour than he had been for a long time, a humour marred only by the failure at Bournsea—that job was the more exasperating because they were probably within an ace of getting the right man—Gideon saw a rakish-looking sports car following him in his driving mirror. He had never noticed the car before. The fair-haired driver had a nice-looking blonde beside him and she was sitting a little too close for safety and freedom of movement. His mind spurred by the afternoon conference, Gideon found himself wondering what could be done to lessen accidents at their source: the driver. This chap, for instance.

This chap swung out near some traffic lights, put on a burst of speed, and roared past Gideon's black Wolseley. It would not be true to say that he was driving carelessly; just over-confidently.

The blonde had stared at Gideon as they had passed.

"Know who that was?" asked Keith Ryman.

"He looked like a heavy-weight champion," said Helen facetiously.

"That's Gideon of the Yard," Ryman informed her,

smiling as he stared ahead. "He's hit the headlines lately, and given me one or two ideas. But he's just a thickhead, like the rest of these cops. Something nasty will happen to him one day. Now, pet, about this nurse-maid job. I know you won't like it, but you'll have to lump it. The thing is, do you know how to handle kids well enough to seem genuine?"

"Keith, *darling*, cooed Helen, "I've three sisters and a brother, all younger than me. It wasn't until I got away from home last year that I stopped being a real little mother. I can look after kids all right. How long do you think I'll have to do it, though?"

"Perhaps a week."

"Oh, I can stand a week. How old is the kid?"

"About a year."

"Not even house-trained," Helen complained. "Well, provided it really means a big cut, darling, I'm in. The only thing is, what will happen if the job falls through?"

"I'll make sure you're not involved, all you have to do is look after the kid," Ryman told her. "The important thing is for you to have a kid about the same age at the cottage for a few days before this one comes—the police will only be on the look-out for women with kids who've just popped up from somewhere."

Helen looked at him, head back and eyes narrowed, lashes sweeping to her cheeks.

"Clever boy," she murmured. "My sister Amy will be glad to have a rest from hers, but I'll be loaded for nearly two weeks. Don't forget I'll be earning that big cut."

"You'll get it," Ryman promised her.

That was as they crossed Hammersmith Broadway, in a stream of traffic. On the kerb of the Underground Station were a constable, young and spruce in a new uniform, and an elderly sergeant. Ryman saw the sergeant, but it did not occur to him that it was Maybell.

158

But he thought of Maybell.

He was sufficiently far ahead in his plans to believe that he could go ahead with all of them in ten days or so.

They were heading for a little bungalow which he owned on the riverside, just above Richmond.

"When am I going to know who the kid is?" asked Helen, as they drove over Barnes Bridge.

"I'll tell you in good time," Ryman answered.

"Don't you trust me?"

"I'm trusting you, aren't I?" He took a hand off the wheel and squeezed her leg, then appeared to give all of his attention to his driving. But he was not doing so. He was thinking of the child he planned to kidnap, also thinking that the important thing with that job, as with everything else, was to cause a distraction. There was a kind of parade ground for perambulators in Hyde Park, where nurses foregather and other children played and the babes in the prams stared at the fascinating colour and movement of their fingers. One, who was regularly in the parade, was Richard Mountbaron, the only child of the extremely wealthy Richard Mountbaron Senior. This parent had inherited both a fortune and the ability to make more money buying and selling real estate; and he had an equally wealthy wife, an American named Charlotte. Ryman had decided not to take a child old enough to talk or run about; a babe in arms could be hidden more easily, would create less fuss, and would create just as much sensation. Every policeman in the country would be on the alert, and if one or two false clues were laid, dozens—perhaps hundreds—could be lured away from the places where he was planning to strike.

Ryman had considered everyone whom he knew with a child of a reasonable age, and had selected the Mountbaron infant as the most suitable.

Next he had to plan the details of the kidnapping. He did not seriously take into account the risk to the child.

13

RIDDELL

One of the angriest and most resentful men in the police force, perhaps the angriest during those few days, was Chief Inspector Thomas Riddell. For some hours after Gideon had rounded on him, Riddell had felt that he could walk out of the Yard and out of the Force; for an hour, he had been very close to doing it. But he was no fool; he had seven more years to go to a full pension, and was living right up to his income. There might be easier and better-paid jobs outside the Metropolitan Police, but he had lost his chance of getting one.

He had told Gideon what he believed was for Gideon's own good; and now, three days after he had arrived in Bournsea, he still could not read the name Gideon or hear it spoken without bridling, although he did not think that anyone else noticed that. He was pretty sure that Hill thought he resented having been sent out of the Yard on this job, but did not suspect a personal grievance.

After the newspaper huzzahs following Micky the Slob's arrest, Riddell had felt even worse; and very bitter. Among other things, being in Bournsea compelled him to cancel two social engagements which his wife had made, and she hadn't been particularly understanding.

To make it worse, Riddell was in poor digs. In the holiday season, accommodation wasn't easy, and all the Yard men had to be fairly close to the police headquarters, housed in an old building at a poor part of the town—the day trippers' end, close to the main pier. Riddell's room was small, it overlooked a back street, and his general view of Bournsea was of countless towels and swim-suits hanging out to dry; the crying of babies; and the noise of radios turned on too loud.

All this was Gideon's fault.

Anger made Riddell apply himself to the child murder problem more single-mindedly than he had approached a case for years. In effect, Gideon had told him that he was a no-good lazy so-and-so, not the realist he had always considered himself. There were two ways in which he could respond; by doing damn-all, which was what Gideon obviously expected, or proving that he could pull his weight with anyone.

By the second day, he had realised that being instrumental in solving this case would be the best way of getting some kind of revenge on Gideon. Hill had assigned him to the odds and ends rather than any specific job; for instance, he was trying to find people who owned a dog without having a licence, and he was still checking the stories of those who claimed to have seen this man and the dog. He had now found three statements saying that the man had gone off on a bicycle, but still there was no good description of the cyclist.

On the Thursday evening, he was eating an evening meal in the company of a holidaymaker, his middle-aged wife and their surprisingly young family, all wanting to see the television. His thoughts were on revenge. What he needed was to discover something no one else had spotted; a completely new angle.

He finished his meal, which hadn't been too bad, went out, and strolled along the promenade from the pier. It was very noisy, for the coaches had not yet taken the day trippers away. The beach was littered with paper, ice-cream wrappers, brown-paper bags and newspapers. The sea was calm and hundreds of people were still bathing although it was after eight o'clock. Riddell was immaculate in his brown suit, wearing a snap-brim trilby, handkerchief poking out of his breast pocket, and tie and socks matching the spotted border of the handkerchief. He was the only well-dressed man in sight. A few girls looked at him, but he was in no mood for thinking about girls who bulged out of sun dresses or low-cut blouses, so he took no notice of them. As he studied the stretch of beach where the man, dog and child had been seen, a thousand people must have been in view. Something of the real magnitude of the task came over him.

"But there must be *some* angle no one's seen," he told himself, and paused to light a cigarette. "Two girls, one six, one seven—both strangled after being assaulted." Riddell felt no repugnance, saw this simply as a case. "Man and dog—dog's saliva and paw-marks, anyhow—in both cases. No footprints, no cycle-tyre prints reported"; he had studied all the reports and the photographs so closely that he would never forget them.

He called to mind everything he had seen and read, and among these was the photograph of the dead child. She had been a pretty kid, but Riddell, who was childless, was looking at the mental image of the photograph only for the help which it might be able to give.

Then he exclaimed: "They both had fine, golden hair!"

He walked on a few steps.

"*That*'s a point," he told himself. "Both very blonde, both blue eyes, both fair complexion, both pretty, even for children. Now he stood and stared out to sea, quite oblivious of a pleasure steamer which was bringing home its load of weary passengers. He went briskly to the copse where the children had been found. Only a small part was still cordoned off. A few gawpers stood by this rope cordon and the two uniformed policemen who were guarding it; uselessly, Riddell thought. He walked briskly up a narrow cutting which led from the beach to the town itself, and caught a bus to the other end of the town and the police station. He went into the office allotted to him and Hill, and was glad that no one was there. He went to a filing cabinet and took out photographs of each of the murdered children.

"Could almost be sisters," he said aloud.

He pulled up a chair and sat down, with a feeling that he might have found what he was seeking. Then he opened the various files on the case; there were dozens of these, the way Hill had set the local men to work was an eye-opener. Riddell knew exactly what he was looking for, and found a file marked: *Children Reported Missing Past Twelve Months*. Inside this were seven photographs of different children, and to each was attached written or typewritten notes. Of the seven, four were blonde, and although they were not really alike, in general appearance there was considerable likeness. Riddell now found himself almost uneasy with excitement. He put aside the cases of the dark-haired children, and read the reports on the others; two had been missed from the beach, one from her home, one had got lost on the way from school to home. In three of the four cases there was a note:

Child states she was offered sweets
by strange man.

Riddell put all seven cases together so that each of
the photographs was side by side. Then he checked the
notes carefully, and decided that in five cases the circumstances were identical except that in three the child
had been allowed to get safely away.

In these, the man had taken the child for a bus ride;
or for a walk; or for a bathe. In no case had the local
police been able to trace the man.

Riddell had enough sense to realise that this was simply because nothing serious had developed; the police
had not had reason to expect murder or assault.

Riddell heard footsteps, and frowned, suspecting that
they were Hill's. They were. Hill opened the door, and
stopped suddenly in the doorway, his big mouth droop-
ing open in surprise. 'If he makes any sarcastic remark
about overtime,' Riddell thought, 'I'll tell him to go to
hell.' He stared up with a curious mixture of defence
and aggression, as Hill came in.

"Hallo, Rid, got anything?"

"Could be," said Riddell.

"Pretty lot of kids." Hill looked at them all. "Could
almost be sisters, couldn't they?"

"That's what I thought. See what I'm driving at?"

"Dunno that I do," said Hill. He sat down on a corner of the small desk, and took out a tobacco pouch
and a patent cigarette-making machine. "Let's have it."

Riddell said: "I think it's possible these four girls"—
he tapped photographs—"were taken away by the man
we're after, but he didn't harm them. It might even
have started harmlessly enough, with just a pervert's
liking for blonde children with long fair hair and blue
eyes. We don't need to go into the motive of the ma-
niacs, do we?"

165

Hill was looking at him steadily.

"Damn good point. Where do we go from there?"

"How many girl children about this age are there these days?"

"Not so many," said Hill, and finished rolling his cigarette, which he seemed to do without a glance at the machine or the tobacco and paper. "We could soon find out, though. Get in touch with every primary and kindergarten school, public and private, and find out. Shouldn't take much more than an hour or two in the morning. Like to handle it?"

"Yes."

"Ta. Any other bright ideas?"

"No," said Riddell, and was not sure whether there was a hint of sarcasm in the remark or not. "I just concentrated, and—but you know how it is."

"Gideon always says that he'd rather spend one hour thinking over a case then ten hours collecting clues," said Hill. "Amazing how often Gee-Gee's right." Riddell did not speak. "I just came in to have a look at the postmen's reports again," he said. "Funny about that dog, too. There just isn't one answering the description as far as we can see—how many dogs did we look at yesterday?"

Riddell grinned.

"Seventy-five."

"Oh, lor'," said Hill, and lit his cigarette; a little flame shot up at the end where a few strands of tobacco hung down, and the smoke was very blue and the smell pungent. "Well, I'd say that this dog's been killed, but why hasn't anyone missed it?" He puffed and blinked, and Riddell knew that he was genuinely deep in thought. Now and again his big jaws moved in a chewing-the-cud kind of motion. "I'd have laid odds that a postman knew every dog on his round."

"Couldn't *be* a postman, could it?" asked Riddell.

"Could be anyone," Hill said musingly, and pondered again. "Can't say we ought to spend much time on that possibility yet, but there's a different angle."

Riddell could not see one, and kept silent.

"The dog would have been about on Saturday, so Saturday's postman would have seen it. It would be missing on Monday. So——"

"Any postman who changed his round this week and started a new one wouldn't know anything about the dogs or people on the round," Riddell put in, suddenly bright-eyed.

"That's it," agreed Hill. "Had that in the back of my mind, I suppose, knew I wanted to think about it a bit more. What kind of "digs" have you got?"

"Bloody awful."

"Bad luck," sympathised Hill. "Mine aren't bad, I've got a room over the Pier Inn. Noisy at night but I don't mind that, my wife always says if I can sleep through my own snoring I can sleep through anything. What about coming over and having a drink? We might think up some more bright ideas between us."

"I'd like to," Riddell said, with almost too much alacrity.

They stayed in the Pier Inn's saloon bar until half past ten, closing time, and each had three whiskies and sodas. Then Riddell walked back to his lodgings. On the way, several cyclists passed him, and he found himself remembering that a cycle had been mentioned in the case. You could never tell: the killer himself might be passing any minute. He thought that several times and, when he reached the front door of the house where he lodged, he stood looking up and down the road, reminding himself that he was getting as bad as Hill and Gideon.

167

A cyclist passed him.

It was George Arthur Smith.

Smith was seeing visions, of girl children with lovely silky golden hair, long hair which was so beautiful beneath one's hand, which seemed to caress him, instead of being caressed by him. He was seeing the faces of girl children, but not girls he had actually known, or had taken out for a bus ride or for a walk, feeding them with sweets, and letting them go some distance from his home. There were girls whom he had never seen; dream girls; and all the same girl, in some strange way.

They all had the same face.

They all had pink, warm, chubby little grubby hands, and they all pointed with a forefinger, the nail of which was slightly bitten.

They all answered to the name of Grace.

He did not even remember that a Grace had once lived next door to him; was dead, yet was alive.

Sometimes they stubbed fingers and noses against the glass of the shop window. Sometimes they breathed on the glass. Sometimes they were giving him money, and he was giving them sweets.

Little Grace.

She lived at 51 Penn Street, not very far from his corner shop.

He cycled past the man standing on the doorstep, without giving him a thought. A policeman was walking along the street further along, and Smith realised that the man was staring at him, but he did not really feel worried, because there was no reason at all to think that he was suspected. In any case it was dark, and he couldn't be seen. He cycled to the shop then, on sudden impulse, went to the corner of Penn Street, and cycled slowly along that. There were several street lights, and one of them was opposite Number 51, but on the other side of the street. The bungalow looked bright and new even in the poor light.

Grace slept in a room at the rear, he knew.

He turned round at the end of the street, and then cycled back, very slowly. He could see little Grace everywhere, and he wanted desperately to stroke her hair. He slowed down, but a couple of young people walked along on the other side of the road, and he quickened the speed of his cycle and went past. He turned towards the shop. He was breathing rather fast now, and just *had* to feel that beautiful silky golden hair. He couldn't help it, he had to go and see Grace.

There was a light in the shop, unusual so late, and then he saw his mother standing on the kerb, looking towards him. As he drew near, she called out in a shrill voice:

"Is that you, Georgie?"

Why did she call him Georgie?

He could hit her.

"Yes, Mum."

"What have you been doing along there?"

"I've just come from the pictures, Mum."

"You don't usually come home that way."

Anger rose up in him, and he jumped off his bicycle and pushed past his mother roughly, wheeled the machine into the shop, and let it fall against a counter; it knocked off some tins of food which were stacked near the edge. His mother came following, and he heard her shooting the bolts of the door. He had longed to go and see Grace, but the spell was broken, and it was *her* fault; the fault of the old woman who now came in and stared at him in a way which he knew was queer.

"George," she said, in an unsteady voice, "there's no need to get cross. I only asked you——"

"I can come home from the pictures any way I like, and it's none of your business," he said roughly. "I'm fed to the teeth with you pestering me with a lot of senseless questions. You lead your life, and I'll lead mine, and that's all about it."

He ate his supper in surly silence, and only grunted 'goodnight'.

When the light in his room had gone out, his mother went to her bed, and knelt down and prayed, because she did not know what to do.

He couldn't be the man; not her Georgie.

He simply couldn't be the man.

But she had seen the way he looked at little Grace, and the way he stroked her hair, and she remembered that first Grace so vividly.

It wasn't a crime to stroke a child's hair, and these days it soothed George. Long, silky, golden hair had fascinated him since he had been very young. From the depths of her memory, Mrs. Smith could see a next-door neighbour's child with hair like spun gold, who had been a bosom friend of her son's. The child had been found hanging from the banisters of her home after a childish game. George had been beside himself with grief, and had taken a long, long time to get over it; for years he had hated girls with that unusual kind of hair.

For some time his mother had believed that these days it soothed him; but was she right?

Keith Ryman lay in his single bed, with Helen in the bed next to him, curled up like a kitten as she always was when asleep. The light from the street lamp in Park Lane was bright enough to shine on her hair, and it touched the mirror in the gilt-framed dressing-table, so that Ryman could just make out his reflection. It

170

was a little after one o'clock, and he had been concentrating for a long time, with so many things buzzing in his mind that he was not sure which ought to have priority. He was aware that there might be snags in all he had planned; he must get the police searching for the baby before there was any attempt at ransom, for instance. He might decide not to go ahead with the ransom. Helen wanted the twenty-five thousand he said he was going to demand for the baby, but it was only chicken feed, and might carry a big risk. There'd be plenty for Helen out of the bank job. They could send the baby back—provided they could make sure that the kidnapping couldn't be traced back to them.

Rather than that, they must kill and bury it.

Would Helen be like Rab Stone? Soft-hearted.

There was another snag over the two policemen, the kind of thing one sensed but could not understand. Gideon as a victim was in the back of his mind, but Ryman had gone no farther than thinking it a good idea. Its weakness might be that the police would certainly exert themselves for Gideon, and he did not want to goad them too far.

"Just get them running round in circles," he told himself.

He went very still and stared up at the ceiling, for he had seen a real snag. He was going to get two men to kill two coppers; two crook-murderers who would have to be paid. Either of them might talk; what was more, each had been inside, or at least associated with crime, and each was known to hate a particular policeman. The police would go straight to these obvious suspects and they would be able to say *who* had paid them. Not him, of course, nor Stone, not even Si Mitchell, but a go-between. All the same, it wasn't safe. The police might get on to Si, and if Si was frightened enough he might name Rab Stone.

This was how fools got caught: not looking far enough ahead.

He gave a snort of laughter. Helen started, and shifted her position a little, but did not wake up. He began to laugh in earnest, and smothered the sound beneath the sheet. The solution to this was obvious once one thought about it.

The men who hate Maybell and Archer must *not* kill the policeman; someone else, who had no known motive, would do that. The police would immediately go for the obvious suspects, who would protest they had nothing to do with it. But supposing each had been lured to the murder spot; once it was known that they had been there, the police would simply laugh when they said they had been framed. And the police would feel positive that they had the right men.

Ryman stopped laughing.

"It's golden," he muttered, inspired by his own brilliance. "Golden!"

Then he thought: "But we can't take chances with other people. I'll have to do one job, Rab the other."

He thought in silence for a few minutes, and went on:

"That's it. It'll have to be after dark. We'll fix the cops next Thursday. We'll snatch the baby on Friday morning, tennish, and fix the bank van Friday afternoon, two o'clock, the time it always leaves."

He turned over, drew the bedclothes up to his chin, and closed his eyes; five minutes afterwards he was fast asleep.

Less than half a mile away, the Mountbaron family slept, the baby in a dressing-room next to his parents.

* * *

Little Grace slept at 51 Penn Street, but Smith was restless.

London slept, and so did Bournsea.

14

TWO MOTHERS

Gideon woke next morning soon after seven o'clock, and Kate turned over and began to flicker her eyes. "I'll get some tea," Gideon said, and went downstairs, yawning. It was very bright outside. The first thing on his mind was the Bournsea affair, for the newspapers screamed headlines that a child had been attacked at Seaham, fifty miles along the coast; that was true, but it wasn't connected; the local police had already caught the man. The prominence of this story betrayed summer's shortage of news, as well as the fact that public anxiety was really aroused.

Gideon had to make himself concentrate on the things Kate had suggested about his draft proposals; good, sound comment, to make it as simple as he could. He wouldn't have a chance to plead a case like a barrister in court, she's reminded him.

"I think you'll just have to make a précis in a page or two, dear, a summary to make everyone sit up. You'll need all this to support it, but—well, I suppose the truth is, you've got to frighten everyone who can help."

Frighten everyone; that was it. And make the Home

Secretary listen. Gideon still felt uneasy about the Home Office reaction to his Sunday statement, but it was a quiescent anxiety now.

He reached the office early, and decided that this was a day to behave as the acting AC and to leave Bell to take over on his own as stand-in Commander. He went along to the AC's office, and found pencils sharpened, inkwell filled, a clean pad, everything that he could need ready; including an array of morning newspapers one upon the other. Either Rogerson had been lucky, or knew how to train staff. Within fifteen minutes, Gideon was fidgety, wanting to know what was going on. After half an hour, he found it almost impossible to sit there and go through the mass of administrative papers, as well as report upon report at AC level.

At ten o'clock, his own 'case report' pushed aside, he stood up. He had allowed Bell plenty of time; it would no longer look as if he couldn't trust the CI. As he opened the door, a telephone rang in Miss Sharp's room, and a moment later one rang on his desk. He went back to answer it.

"Will you speak to Superintendent Hill, sir? He's been talking to Chief Inspector Bell, and would like to have a word with you if you can spare a minute."

"I'll talk to him." Gideon stood very still, staring at the window, seeing not the plane trees waving gently, nor the roof of the London County Hall, but the beach and the blue sea, a fair-haired child and a dog.

"You're through," Miss Sharp said.

"That you, Hippo?"

"Yes, but not with the news you want yet," said Hill, promptly. "We haven't got any farther, George, except in one way. I cursed you for sending me that drip Riddell but he's come up with a good one. Got a mind if

175

he can be made to use it. Did you kick him down here?"

"Yes."

"Thought as much. He used to bare his teeth when he heard the name Gideon. Anyhow, he——"

Hill did not waste words.

". . . and he's talking to the headmasters of the different schools, there are twenty-three in the district," he went on. "We're going to have each school watched at lunchtime and this afternoon, and every child with that kind of fair hair followed. Right?"

"Nice work." It was first-class. "Might be more in Riddell than I realised."

"Thanks, AC," said Hill. "How do you like being upstairs?"

"If I don't like it any more at the end of a month, I'd rather be back on the beat," Gideon said. "Talked much to Bell?"

"He's on the ball."

"Fine," said Gideon.

The call had cheered him up a great deal. He went back to his notes and began to work on them, bearing in mind all that Kate had said. But he needed the fullest possible data before he could put enough kick in the final report.

He sent for Miss Sharp, and began to dictate memoranda and letters; his own voice lulled him into a sense of self-sufficiency, and somehow drowned the cries of those who sought the help of the police.

Little Grace Harrison always stayed at school for lunch, because her mother went out to work, and there was no one home until half past five in the afternoon. A neighbour kept an eye open for any childish troubles, and was always ready to go to the rescue after a

176

cut knee, a grazed hand, or a quarrel with another child. The neighbour's children were all older and able to take care of themselves.

That particular afternoon, she was baking.

That particular afternoon was the one which George Arthur Smith had off duty, if he wanted it, but he stayed in the shop while his mother busied herself out in the garden, where she really enjoyed herself. They had said little to each other that morning, and Smith had given her hardly any thought; he could only think of Grace. He had dreamt of her, he could almost feel the sensuous excitement as he passed his hand over her hair, and in a way she became merged in identity with other children, the two who had started to cry, and whom he had silenced.

She would be home, soon.

It was already half past three.

He sat behind the counter, reading a magazine, and serving the occasional customer. He was near the sweets, and at a spot from which he could see into the street, and the direction from which the children came.

He saw Grace.

And she was on her own.

He put the magazine aside, and swallowed a lump in his throat, then put his hand to one of the big glass jars of toffees, the kind Grace liked. He took a handful out. He looked at the door leading to the back parlour and to his mother, and he wished that she was out. Then he thought suddenly, that he didn't want her to be out, *he* wanted to go off for an hour.

He knew all about Mrs. Harrison, and what time she came home, and that she wouldn't be at the bungalow now. No one would be. He could go along there, as if to deliver some groceries. He could . . .

The child was coming much nearer; skipping lightly. The sun in this golden spell of weather was bright on her hair, making it look like spun gold, and Smith stood up and stared at her, his hands crooked, ready to stroke that hair. He *had* to; he just had to; it drew him as a magnet, and he had no other conscious thought.

Grace came up to the window.

He felt as if he were being stifled by some force beyond his control.

She pressed the palm of her hand against the glass, and then touched it with the tip of her nose, flattening that tip. Her eyes looked huge and blue. He held out the sweets so that she could see them, and she looked up at him in the way that so many girls had looked up at him; trustingly. He gulped again. He beckoned her. She drew away from the window, where there was the smear of her grubby hand and the faint mist from her breath.

Then she turned and walked away, swaying from side to side, until she disappeared.

Smith gritted his teeth.

The little devil, why had she done that?

He pushed the sweets into his pocket, and went to the parlour door, then to the open garden door. His mother was bending down and turning over the soil with a trowel; there was a box of plants by her side.

"I'm going out for an hour," he said, in a voice which he could hardly hear himself, and she took no notice.

"Mother!"

She looked round. "Yes, Georgie?"

Why didn't she stop calling him Georgie?

"I'm going out for an hour. Take over, will you?"

She got to her feet with an effort, for her back got stiff very easily. He could hardly see her face, for instead of grey hair he saw golden, instead of lined cheeks he saw smooth ones.

"All right," she said. "Where are you going?"

178

"*Never mind where I'm going, I can go where I like!*" he shouted at her, and turned round, strode across the little dark parlour and into the shop, and then to the street. Grace was out of sight. He had to catch up with her, and make her talk to him. He had those sweets, he would take her for a bus ride. She was bound to like a bus ride. He quickened his pace as he felt the attraction, a kind of compulsion which he could not resist; it had never been like this before, never so powerful and insistent.

He did not look round to see his mother in the shop doorway.

He turned the corner, and saw Grace, opening the gate which led to the bungalow.

His mother saw him turn the corner.

She closed her eyes and covered her face with her hands and stood there for several seconds. Then she turned round. The telephone was in a corner, a black shiny futuristic beetle. She went to it, slowly, and her footsteps seemed to drag. She touched it. There were tears in her eyes and trickling down her cheeks, and she hated doing what she knew she must do.

She said, as if praying: "If it isn't Georgie, it won't hurt him, and if it is . . ."

"It can't be my Georgie!"

She clutched the telephone, lifted it, and then with a misshapen forefinger began to dial 999. She did not know what she would say to the police, but she had to tell them about the dog and about her fear.

They would only put Georgie away for a few years, whatever he had done.

She must not take the chance that he might have time to harm another child.

That was when she realised that she was positive of the truth about her son.

Grace knew that the back door of the bungalow was always unlocked, so that she could go in and get a drink, or help herself to some biscuits and a slice of cake. She was swinging her arms and her shoulders, rather more bored than usual because she was alone. The children who usually walked home with her had been kept late. It had been fun coming home at first, and she had been warned and had solemnly observed her kerb drill, but it was dull now.

She went into the kitchen, drank some milk, spilt a little and wiped it up, then went into her small bedroom, where she kept her dolls; whenever she was lonely, she went to her dolls. She picked up a black piccaninny with a big, shiny face and eyes which opened and closed, and a small, battered rag doll. She began to talk to both, gradually warming up to a kind of enthusiasm.

She heard a sound, looked round, and saw the man from the corner shop looking at her. She did not notice the strange gleam in his eyes, but did see that his hand was held out towards her, and there were sweets in it.

"I haven't got any money," she announced.

"That—that doesn't matter."

"Oo!" Her eyes lit up, she sprang towards him, and then remembered that he had corrected her yesterday, and hurriedly she said: "Thank you very much, please." She took a toffee, felt his hand, and then felt him touch her hair. People often smoothed down her hair, and called her Goldilocks.

The man's hand was pressing heavily on the back of her head, and he was drawing her to him. She looked at him, not really afraid, but puzzled.

"I'm going to take you for a long bus ride," he said, thickly. "I'm going to take you ——"

This was a dream come true! A dream, a golden dream, everything he wanted, everything——

A shadow darkened the doorway of this room, and a big man entered. Behind him was another man, almost as massive. Smith jumped away from the girl child, and backed into a corner, while terror was born in his eyes.

"I just came for the weekly order," he gabbled. "I came for the weekly order, that's all. I'm the grocer, I came for the weekly order!"

"We'll have a talk about it, shall we?" asked the first big man. "I'm Detective Sergeant Whaley, of the Criminal Investigation Department." Whaley smiled at the child, and then the neighbour came, hurrying because she had been summoned without being told why.

"Is she all right?"

"She's perfectly all right," the CID man assured her. "She won't even know what it's all about. Take her away now, will you? There's no need for her to see us take this man off."

"I came to collect the order," gabbled Smith. "I forgot Mrs. Harrison would be out, I just forgot, all I came for was the order."

"What order did you go to the beach for on Saturday?" Whaley asked in a hard voice.

"When it did break, everything broke at once," Hill said to Gideon on the telephone. "But Riddell's idea was the one which really did the trick. We got on to this Harrison child through her school, like we did fifty or sixty others, but then things began to tie up. There's been a change of postmen on this route, and we had a word with the chap who was on it last week; he de-

scribed that dog to a T. It was Smith's. Several neighbours said they hadn't seen the dog since Saturday,
once we asked them the specific question. It added up
even better when we found out that Smith often goes
to the beach, and spends a lot of time there, and is
always giving sweets to children. We knew we had him
all right," went on Hill, for once very garrulous, "but
it was nearly one of those jobs which other people solve
for us. Smith's mother had suspicions, she was actually
calling us when Smith was being taken away from the
bungalow. No more harm done, thank God, and that's
lifted the shadow off Bournsea."

"Couldn't be better news," said Gideon. "How about
spending a few days down there tidying the job up?
That's if your wife won't mind."

Hill chuckled.

"And keep Riddell there for a day or so, but send
the other chaps back," Gideon said. "Thanks, Hippo."

"Okay, Gee-Gee," Hill said. "It's a load off my mind
all right."

Gideon put the receiver down, pushed his chair back,
and went across to the window. It could hardly be a
more pleasant scene, for the sun was rippling on the
smooth water of the Thames, gaily covered river-boats
were sailing in each direction, even the London County
Hall looked more beautiful. Just out of sight were the
Houses of Parliament, with the Home Secretary's Office . . . After a few minutes, he sighed, scratched his
head, and returned to the desk, where dozens of letters
waited for signing.

"If you ask me, Miss Sharp could run this office as
well as any A.C.," Gideon said, and then grinned. "Better not tell Rogerson that!"

He sat down and began to sign.

* * *

Mrs. Mountbaron, of whom Gideon had read several times in the national press, for she was wealthy enough to be news, had last been in the headlines when the baby had been born. She lived in a modest nine-roomed apartment in a big new building overlooking Park Lane and Hyde Park. Only three hundred yards away was the small apartment, looking over the same green pleasance, where Ryman lived.

She had never heard of Ryman.

She was looking at her only child, who was sitting in a low chair which could be wheeled across the room, beating the tray in front of it with podgy hands, eyes gleaming and cheeks aglow. If anything, Clarissa was too fat, but the doctors and experts ridiculed any such suggestion, saying that once she began to crawl and walk the puppy fat would melt away. Certainly she could not look healthier and happier.

It was a long, gracious room, with a wide window and a small balcony. The Nanny was on the balcony, collecting some baby clothes which had been spread out in the sun. A girl in her late teens, she came in while pressing a woollen coatee against her cheeks.

"They're so dry they'll hardly need airing, but I'd better put them in the cupboard, I suppose. Will you be all right with her for ten minutes, ma'am?"

"I think I can manage," Mrs. Mountbaron said dryly.

It seemed a shame to pick the child up, and perhaps disrupt this spell of bliss. In two minutes or in ten Clarissa would get a little fractious, and she would want to pick her up, while Nanny would fight to prevent her; Nanny was undoubtedly right, but it seemed a pity that a child couldn't do exactly what it felt like doing for the first year or so of its life.

The mother leaned back on a couch, her legs up, a dark-haired, most attractive, olive-skinned woman.

Close to her side was a small table, and on this a photograph of her husband, with her and the child; the perfect family group. Mrs. Mountbaron did not consciously think this as she glanced at the photograph, but she was basking in a kind of happiness which had seemed dreamlike years ago. Two years married, and hardly a ripple had marred contentment.

She almost purred.

Clarissa suddenly gave a sharp, urgent cry, for no reason at all except that this mood of bliss was passing.

"Nanny says you must learn to stay put even when you don't want to," the mother said, and didn't stir. "Let's see how long I can let you."

Five minutes later, when Clarissa was red in the face with crying, she could stand it no longer, jumped up from the couch, bent down, and lifted her child. She crossed to it as tears streamed down its face, but Clarissa was quiet now that she was cradled in eager arms. The mother took it to the window to have a look at the park, pointed with one hand, and said:

"You see the trees down there, and that patch of grass, my precious? That's where Nanny will take you again in the morning, and I'll wave to you."

Nanny came in.

"*Really*, Mrs. Mountbaron," she protested, "you'll never teach Clarissa to have self-control if you insist on picking her up the moment she cries. I would be doing less than my duty if I didn't keep reminding you."

"You do your duty wonderfully," Mrs. Mountbaron said. "Why don't you go and get her bath ready, I'll bring her in ten minutes."

The Nanny gave up trying to look severe.

"Now over there," said Mrs. Mountbaron to the heedless child, "is Buckingham Palace, where the Queen and Prince Philip live, with Princess Anne and the Duke of Cornwall, sometimes known as Prince Charles. You can't see the Palace from here, silly. Up there is Marble Arch . . ."

15

THURSDAY

"I don't see how anything can go wrong," Keith Ryman said. "We've got it all laid on, Rabbie, with a minimum of people involved. Just you and me, Archie, Si Mitchell, and Helen. I've been over every little point a dozen times, and I don't see what can go wrong. Can you?"

"Looks okay to me, " Rab agreed, "except——"

He broke off.

"Now's the time to say if you've got doubts or if you can see any weakness," Ryman said, very sharply. "It's Wednesday, and we go into action tomorrow, copping the cops. We take the Mountbaron kid first, half past ten in the morning. You distract the nurse's attention in Hadden Street, got that clear? I'll take the kid, Archie will be at the wheel, and Helen will be waiting down at the cottage to look after things. It'll go like clockwork. Any complaint about that?"

"There's always a chance that someone will be passing, but it should be okay," Stone conceded. His shiny face and polished hair made his head look rather smaller than it was, and although he smiled, he could not remove the uncertainty from his eyes.

"Then what's the worry?"

"It's doing the four jobs in a row."

"That's the very idea, what's got into you?"

"It isn't anything in particular," Stone said, hesitantly, "it's just——"

"You don't like the idea of killing Maybell. That it?" Ryman was hard-voiced.

"I don't give a damn about rubbing him out if it will do any good, but——"

"You've been in on this from the beginning," Ryman said. "There isn't an angle we haven't discussed. It's too late to start making objections now, and don't forget it. You don't seem to have it straight. I'll be waiting for Maybell when he turns the corner of his street, at ten-fifteen tonight. He's doing a two-till-ten turn. It'll be dark where I'll be. I'll just let him have it. And Charlie Daw will be doing a job close-by at the identical time, that's laid on, isn't it?"

"Yes, that's okay."

"And you'll go to Archer's house at the same time—as it's five miles away, that's no problem. He'll answer the door himself, and you'll give it to him before he can ask who you are. Thursday's the right night, he's always on his own—his fiancée spends Thursdays home with her mother. What can go wrong with that?"

"Nothing, I suppose."

"Worried about the holdup?" Ryman demanded. "We'll have the van away from the City and over the river in ten minutes, and we'll have it unloaded and dumped ten minutes after that. We know just where to plant the money, we've got five different places ready. The police will be so busy with the Mountbaron kid and the two copper killings that we'll catch them on the wrong foot. We've checked every point and every detail, we even know how it will go minute by minute. Let's hear your argument against it, Rab, and if it isn't pretty good, forget it."

Stone shrugged.

"Well, let's have it, don't stand there like a goon."

"It's just——" Stone waved his hands, helplessly. "It's just that we seem to be tempting fate, Keith. We want *four* different jobs to go right. I could go all the way if it was one or even two, but the chance of something going wrong in four different jobs is four times greater than it is in one. That's logical, isn't it?"

"It's logical," agreed Ryman. "It's true, too. But four times none are none, aren't they?"

Stone said: "I suppose you're right."

"What is it?" Ryman demanded, in a cold voice. "Want to cry off?"

"That's the last thing I'd do. The snatch and the van job, they're fine, but the police jobs——"

"You don't get the point," said Ryman. "It seems to me that you never have got the point. It's the police and the child jobs which get them by the short hairs. Look what's happened in this past ten days. They cut down on everything else and concentrated on Micky the Slob. Why was that? Micky's a small-time crook, isn't he, he was never really dangerous. Usually they'd put him on the list and wait for him. They detailed one man—*one man*, Rab—to look after him, that's how important it was to them; then he killed that police sergeant, and they put hundreds of men on the job. They neglected everything else and concentrated on Micky the Slob. You know it as well as I do. The police can't be in two places at the same time, so all the little crooks came out and did what they wanted for a day or so. Perhaps I'm exaggerating, but the principle's right. You take it from me, with three major jobs all in different parts of London, the rest of London will look like Trafalgar Square early on a Sunday morning as far as the police are concerned. Even big-mouth Gideon will be out on the search. They'll just keep a skeleton staff for routine, and they won't have any idea about the bank van job. Got that? They wouldn't have in any case—but on Friday they won't even have time to remember that there are such things as holdups."

Ryman paused.

Then he asked: "How about it, Rab. Convinced? Or will you drop out, and let me get someone else?"

"I'm with you," Rab Stone said. "I'm just a bit nervy, that's all. It's a damned big conception, Keith, it's difficult for me to grasp it."

"You'll grasp it when the cash comes," Ryman assured him.

Gideon was walking about the AC's office, one hand in his pocket, the other grasping his empty pipe, and waving in the air or stabbing to emphasise a point. Miss Sharp sat silent, and her pencil moved with the rapidity of the quickest male stenographers at the Yard.

". . . another aspect of this situation, emphasising its gravity, is the consequence of a mass-scale search. Take, for instance, the facts relating to the concentration of forces, on the docks in the NE Division only last week. Men were drafted in from all neighbouring Divisions and from Central Office. The Central Division and neighbouring divisions were denuded of staff. Normally they work at about sixty-five percent of full complement, but when a large number of men was temporarily transferred to special duty, the actual complement on normal duty was lowered to fifty per cent or less.

"Paragraph.

"The rest of the men were concentrating on the docks.

"Moreover, seventy per cent of the River Division's

craft and operative men were also concentrated on the docks.

"The immediate result appeared to be satisfactory; the wanted man was apprehended, without serious damage to the ship on which he had taken refuge, no one was injured, and the necessary arrests were made. However, much damage and possible serious injury would have been done but for the voluntary information lodged by the woman Rose Lemman.

"Paragraph.

"Before the situation in the Divisions concerned was restored to normal, that is to sixty-five per cent of full complement, the incidence of crime in the affected Divisions increased by forty-nine per cent over normal. Many forms of indictable crime showed a sharp increase during that period only. Housebreaking, pilfering from other sections of the docks, shoplifting, dipping——"

Miss Sharp looked up.

"Dipping?"

"Pickpocketing," said Gideon, and hesitated. "No, that's not right. Dipping. Picking of pockets." He scowled. "Cut out dipping, and put it this way: Shoplifting, bag-snatching and similar crimes increased in such a way due entirely to the fact that it was impossible to cope with the emergency requirements for a large force of officers in one place, and to control the rest of the Divisions properly. Most members of the criminal fraternity are very quick-witted, and don't miss many chances.

"A similar phenomenon——" Gideon paused, considered Miss Sharp's bowed, greying head, and then went on: "Yes, that's right, a similar phenomenon was evident at Bournsea during the weekend in which a concentration of officers was required. Housebreaking and burglary increased by forty-one per cent over the average for the previous weekend, and thirty-eight per cent over the number for the corresponding weekend in each of the previous three years. There are indications that some of the Bournsea crimes were committed by London criminals who realised what would happen, and made a special trip to Bournsea.

"These and other indications make it, in my view, beyond all doubt that while the staffing of the CID—spell that out—and the uniformed branches, remains at its present unsatisfactory level, very grave consequences may follow whenever a large concentration of men is required. A survey of the concentrations so needed in the Metropolitan Police area alone in the past twelve months has been——"

"I'll fill in that figure later," Gideon decided, after a moment's pause, and then looked at his watch; it was five minutes to eleven. "We deserve a break after that lot, Miss Sharp, I've never dictated so much in my life!" He paused again. "Do you have any difficulty in taking it down?"

"No more than usual," said Miss Sharp, politely. "Would you like tea or coffee this morning?"

"Tea," answered Gideon, and grinned at her departing back.

After tea, he went into his own office, and found Bell on the telephone, Culverson on a second, a third ringing, a Chief Inspector waiting for Bell, a pile of papers six inches high on Bell's desk, awaiting attention, and indications that Bell was finding the pressure too hard. Culverson had a harassed look, too.

Gideon picked up the telephone which was ringing.

"Gideon," he announced.

"Thank Gawd you're back," said Hopkinson of NE. "How long are you going to hide yourself in that smart office?"

"What's the trouble, Hoppy?"

"Picked up a bit of information which might be helpful," Hopkinson told him, "but it doesn't affect me much, and I thought it ought to be passed on to CD. Remember Charlie Daw?"

"Of course I do."

"Well, one of my Divisional chaps was over there with some friends for a few days, and says that Charlie's been casing a house in Woodside Road, Hammersmith. A wholesale jeweller lives there and he takes a lot of his jewels home with him. He has a big safe at the house and prefers not to leave it at the lock-up shop. Care to tip Benson off?"

Benson, the Chief Superintendent in charge of CD Division, which included Hammersmith, was notoriously a law unto himself, and difficult to approach.

"I'll fix it," Gideon promised.

"That's what I like to hear," said Hopkinson. "George, I don't want to swell you up with pride, but the trouble with old Bell and that sergeant is that they can't say a thing like that. The best they can do is 'I'll see what we can arrange'. No authority, if you see what I mean. Don't mind me chipping in with that, I hope?"

"Glad to know," said Gideon. "I can see it's a weakness. Thanks, Hoppy. I'll be seeing you. Oh, wait a minute! Rose Lemman's coming up after her eight-day remand today, isn't she?"

"Not to mention Micky the Slob."

"We don't need to think twice about Micky," Gideon said, "but it might be a good idea to allow Rose Lemman bail, if she can put up a bit. If she applies, I shouldn't oppose it, just leave it to the beak."

"Good idea," agreed Hopkinson.

He did not say the obvious; that in five minutes he had seen two aspects of Gideon's particular genius for his job: the authority with which he could speak and act, and the knowledge he had of the mood of the criminal fraternity. If leniency was shown to Rose, a kind of sympathy-bond would spring up between police and criminals. It might not mean a great deal, but would help a little. It might even lead to a few squeals.

Gideon called Benson, and made it seem as if he himself had seen Charlie Daw.

"Grateful for that, Gee-Gee, thanks a lot." Benson was a brisk man. "I'll have the house specially watched for the next night or two, Daw won't get away with anything again."

"That sergeant who caught him still around?"

"Maybell? Yes," answered Benson. "Very sound man. He's just decided to keep on until he's sixty-five, and I didn't discourage him. How is the fight with the Home Office going on?" Benson only just succeeded in concealing his laugh.

"So-so," said Gideon; that was his stock answer.

So the place which Charlie Daw had been told was a cinch, and which he was to raid tomorrow, Thursday, night, would be specially watched by the police.

Detective Officer Dave Archer's one serious weakness during that particular period was his eagerness to leave promptly on certain evenings, and also his tendency to haunt the telephone at particular times of day; true, he did not spend much time talking to his fiancée, but he was not concentrating wholly on his job.

That Thursday evening he was, however, when making a report on an arrest made during the afternoon—of a barrow boy known to have stolen two cases of oranges. It was half past five, and he did not greatly mind whether he left at six o'clock or seven, for this was Drusilla's night with her mother, and his for reading up the police manual. When he was called to the telephone, he expected it to be a message from one of the officers out on duty.

"Hallo, darling," Drusilla greeted.

" 'Silla!"

"I've just got home, and mother's decided that she would like to go and see that French film we saw on Monday," Drusilla said. "I wondered if by any chance you would be able to find me a sandwich and a cup of tea if I came round to the flat for an hour or so."

He could picture her eyes, laughing at him.

He glanced round quickly, and no one was within earshot.

"Sounds gloriously improper," he said. "Wonderful! You couldn't call in at a Corner House and get something for the sandwich, could you?"

"Love to! All right, darling, see you soon."

Archer finished his report with surprising speed, and was at his small two-roomed flat in a house near Paddington, not far from the Edgware Road, at twenty to seven, before his Drusilla arrived.

As always, she looked clear-eyed and fresh, and to him, quite lovely; she yielded against his body when he held her, as if there was nothing more she wanted.

They were to be married in a month's time.

That Thursday evening, the Mountbarons spent together, looking at television, reading during the shows they didn't like, alert for any sound from the nursery.

There was none.

"The whole thing is taking shape now," Gideon said to Kate. "I shall do two reports, a brief one as you suggested, as an appetiser, and a fully documented one.

194

The figures are worse even than I thought. Every Division has come up with facts and figures quicker than I expected, too; they're all sick to death with just scraping along. It's a blurry funny thing——"

He saw Kate smile, quickly, and knew why: no one could ever get used to massive Gideon saying 'blurry', instead of 'bloody', but it had started when his first child had started imitating him, nearly thirty years ago, and he had realised that he must watch his language.

"—that I didn't realise just how bad the situation was until I talked to the chap from Fleet Street, and he put it into words. In fact it's worse than he made out. If we could get a ten per cent increase in staff we'd work miracles in this city." He was glowing with enthusiasm. "We'd keep a lot more chaps on from sixty to sixty-five, too; they'd be able to release younger chaps for the active work. The way this thing is shaping, we'll really have a case, even for a one-eyed Home Sec."

"How is Popple now?" asked Kate. "He really started it."

"Keen as mustard. Looks in every day with some suggestion or other—and the Old Man came in twice today, to talk about a draft of the memo I've just shown you, about the effect of drawing men from one Division to help another. That shook him. We've had nineteen of these concentrated search cases in a year. Don't realise it at the time, do you?"

"I know there are a lot of them," Kate said, and looked at him very thoughtfully. "Think you'll want to go on until you're sixty-five, not sixty, George?"

He hesitated.

"What do you think would be best?"

"I suppose we'll have to wait until it's nearer the time to decide," Kate said, "and that's not for eight years. But I've always had a dream that we might take

195

a really long trip before we're too old to enjoy new places and things. I mean, a *really* long trip."

"We will, if we can afford it," Gideon answered her.

He wondered how many Yard men who worked past the sixty mark did so because they needed the money, and how many of them did so because the job held them so tightly. He knew that Kate feared the unrelenting hold of the job on him more than the shortage of money.

So did he.

16

ATTACKS

Only two and a half miles away, and at that very minute, Sergeant Maybell was turning the corner of the street where he lived. There were some lighted windows and two street lamps, but on the whole the street was very badly lit. It did not occur to him to be nervous, but he knew that women and young girls disliked walking along here at night on their own, and he knew also that there were many more cases of assault and attempted rape than a few years ago. That was one of the reasons why he had decided not to resign next year. He walked with the long, easy stride of a man who was physically very fit; he kept his bicycle at the station, which was only ten minutes' walk away, because he enjoyed walking to and from his work. He did not think very seriously about the lighting in the street, or in the fact that the doorways and the porches might hold a prowling man; they were at least as likely to hold a cuddling couple. Maybell, who was too old to be a cynic and too experienced to be surprised, was whistling a tune that was at least forty years old.

He heard a sound behind him.

He turned his head.

He felt his helmet tipped over his eyes, and as he twisted round, felt a blow on the back of his head which brought awful pain. It spread from the point of contact down his neck, into his body, into his limbs. He felt himself crumpling up. The second blow, although in fact even harder, did not hurt so much, because he was nearly unconscious already.

His assailant turned and hurried away, and Maybell lay there, dying, for nearly five minutes, before a man turned the corner and saw him.

Charlie Daw, one of the cleverest locksmiths in the business, and who had boasted that he had never found a lock he could not open, proved to his own satisfaction that night that he had not lost his skill while in prison. He had waited for a policeman to pass by on his beat before going to the side door of the jeweller's house. It had a good lock, but was not really difficult. He pushed the heavy door open very cautiously, stepped inside, shone a torch about the dark passageway, and then put it out and closed the door. He knew exactly where the safe was here—beneath the stairs, concealed by wooden panelling on the staircase itself. He listened intently, but heard no sound; obviously the jeweller was out, or upstairs in bed. He studied the panelling, and then found the control switch which released it, and enabled him to slide a door open.

The safe was directly in front of him.

He stepped forward, concentrating his torch light on it, and as he did so, a light flashed on in the hall. He swung round in alarm, and saw three plain-clothes men approaching from three different doors.

"Now turn it in, Charlie," one man said, laconically.

"Who's the so-and-so who squealed?" Charlie demanded, viciously. "Tell me who it was, and one of these days . . ."

* * *

About the same time, Rab Stone went to the Paddington house where David Archer lived, and up to Archer's flat on the second floor. He had seen no light from the street, and that puzzled him, and made him even more uneasy than he usually was over this job. He reached the tiny landing, and pressed the bell. There was a dim yellow light falling on the staircase, but no sound at all.

Speed was the essence of success in a job like this.

No one answered the ring.

He pressed the push again, and heard the ringing inside the flat, but no sound of movement. He backed away from the door, then shone a torch on to a card which was pinned to the door; it was a printed visiting card, and announced: *Mr. David Archer.* There had never been any doubt about this being the right flat.

Where was Archer?

He was always home on Thursday evening; Si Mitchell would not make an elementary mistake about that.

There was a sound downstairs, the opening of the street door, and a moment later the closing of the door and footsteps on the ground-floor passage.

Stone pressed against the wall at the foot of the next flight of stairs up, where the doorway jutted out. He had just a chance to avoid being seen. He felt sure that Archer was approaching, and he could tell from the whistling that the detective was as happy as a man could be.

In fact, Archer had never felt so buoyant. He had just seen Drusilla home, spent twenty minutes talking to her and her mother, and was now positive that there would be no obstacle or difficulty put in the way of their marriage. In four weeks' time it would be Mr. and Mrs. Dave Archer, much sooner than he had first anticipated. From the moment of meeting Drusilla it had been like falling downhill; he had been quite unable to stop himself from becoming more and more obsessed with love for her. Four weeks: and in that time they had to decide whether to come and start their married life in this poky flat, or find a larger one; whether to spend a small fortune on a continental honeymoon, or to have a few days at the south coast and the rest of the two weeks—his holiday for the year,—in London.

He thought: "The one certain thing is that we'll need a double bed!"

He grinned, stopped whistling, took out his keys, and selected the front-door key. He began to hum. Metal scraped on metal, and he pushed the door open. It creaked. He groped for the light switch, and as he did so, heard a movement from his right. He had not seen or heard anyone there before, but now he turned, bewilderingly swift with his reflex actions.

He saw the dark figure of a man launching himself forward, and in the pale yellow light saw a knife in the man's hand.

He swept his right arm round.

His elbow cracked into the other's face, but at the same moment he felt a searing pain in his back, between the ribs, near the heart. It was an awful, frightening moment. He hissed, trying to tense his whole body and so prevent the pain from becoming worse, still trying to protect himself. He felt himself falling. He had strength left, and he shouted the one word: *"Help!"* and he buffeted the man again, striking him somewhere about the head.

"Help," he tried to shout again, but there was very little sound from his lips. "Help," he whispered as he sank down, frightened, helpless, aware of movement

and near-by sounds, aware of another searing pain in his back.

His breath hissed inwards again.

He thought he heard someone call from the flat above. He did hear footsteps. There was still pain; it was not new, but the same one as before. It seemed to be spreading. Footsteps thundered on the stairs, he heard a door slam, then saw light appear above his head. The man who lived in the flat above came hurrying down, while another man came up from the flat below.

Outside, Stone was gasping for breath, holding the knife, running desperately to the motor cycle which was parked around the corner. He ought to be walking steadily. He ought to be taking this quite calmly, but he could not. As he neared the corner he was in great fear, in case someone turned it and bumped into him, and he actually held the knife ready to use in emergency. He reached the motor cycle, and began to wipe the bloodied blade with a piece of rag he had brought with him for the purpose. He thrust the knife between his trousers and belt, then straddled the machine. Although it could not be more than a minute or two since he had left Archer, he felt terrified in case the police were summoned by a call to 999; they could reach any given spot in sixty seconds.

"So you got him," said Ryman, with deep satisfaction. "Sure he's dead?"

"I didn't have time to feel his pulse, but——"

"Did he see you?"

"Didn't have a chance," Stone assured him. He had revived his spirits with a whisky and soda and, looking back, was prepared to belive that he had done a perfect job. If he could believe Keith, Keith had, too.

"Then the first half of the job's gone right," said Ryman. "That's fine, Rabbie, old boy, what did I tell you? You stay here for the night, and Helen will give us both alibis. There isn't a thing that can go wrong."

"What do we want alibis for, no one can suspect us, can they?" Stone demanded.

"You've never said a truer word," said Ryman. "Don't be so touchy." He slit open a new packet of cigarettes, lit one, and went on musingly: "Charlie Daw was out at Hammersmith, and Cartwright was doing a job at Paddington. By a remarkable coincidence, there will be squeaks about each of them tomorrow morning."

Stone didn't answer.

Ryman said roughly: "What the hell's the matter with you now? I'm sick to death of you looking as if the bell's going to ring with the police any moment."

"Keith," said Stone, and stopped. "Keith," he went on, "if they know who did the jobs, or if they think they know, it won't draw the police off on a big manhunt, will it? They'll just pick up Charlie Daw and Cartwright."

Ryman actually backed a pace away; and there was the hush of dismay before he said gruffly:

"We won't send the squeaks through, that's all, we'll leave the police to find out for themselves."

But his voice was hoarse with the shock of realising that he had been so blinded by the brilliance of the idea.

"And they won't have any idea who's taken that baby," he said, more sharply. "That's certain."

* * *

Gideon was actually asleep when the telephone bell rang. It was a long time since he had been roused by night regularly, but the habit of years quickly reasserted itself, and he was awake on the instant. He heard Kate gasp; so she was also awake. The telephone was by the side of the bed near the light; he hitched himself up and stretched out for it, then put on the light.

"Gideon."

"Hi, Gee-Gee." There was no mistaking the bright, perky Cockney voice. This was Lemaitre, for years Gideon's chief assistant, more recently the Chief Superintendent on night duty at the Yard—in effect Gideon's counterpart by night. "Sorry to wake you up, old cock, but you'd tear us to bits in the morning if I hadn't. Nasty show tonight."

Gideon was sitting erect, and Kate was looking at him, thick dark hair in curlers, her face a little shiny with night creams.

"Let's have it, Lem."

Lemaitre told him . . .

". . . and Maybell's a goner, must have died instantaneously. Archer's got a good chance, they say—knife just missed his heart. Lost a lot of blood and he'll need watching, but with luck he'll be about again in a few weeks. The devil of it is, who'd have a cut at a couple of coppers on the same night? That's the question."

"Send to the Division, pick up Charlie Daw——" Gideon began.

"Couldn't have been Charlie," declared Lemaitre. "He was picked up in Hammersmith on another job. We know the time that Maybell got his, Charlie simply couldn't have done it, which is a spot of luck for Charlie Daw, because if there had been time I'll bet we'd have had him on toast for it. What do you intend to do, George? Coming over?"

"Yes, right away."

"Still the same old pioneering spirit," said Lemaitre, and it was easy to imagine his grin. "Okay, old cock, I'll have a cuppa char ready for you."

"Don't go," urged Gideon. He was staring at the window, the lamplight and the reflection of Kate's face, but he did not really notice Kate. "Daw was near Maybell, and we had a squeak that he would be in Hammersmith. Don't go." He stared tensely as he tried to see the association clearly in his mind. "Daw always swore he'd get Maybell when he came out, didn't he? And wasn't there a whisper a few weeks ago, after Archer had stopped the man Cartwright in the smash and grab, that Cartwright's father said he'd get Archer?"

"Gorblimey!" Lemaitre gasped.

"Put a call out for Cartwright, and then keep both him and Daw on ice for me," Gideon urged. "I'll be there in half an hour." He rang off, pushed the bed-clothes back, then belatedly glanced at Kate. "Sorry, Kate, but two of our chaps have been attacked tonight, I'd better go and see what's doing myself. No need for you to get up, I can get all I want at the Yard." He squinted at the mantelpiece clock. "It's only just turned twelve, early yet."

Kate didn't say 'Must you go?' and even when he was leaving the bedroom, did not adjure him to be careful, but he knew exactly what was in her mind. The telephone had not disturbed any of the children, and he crept downstairs with unnecessary stealth, went out, and walked briskly to the garage near by, a lock-up which was awkward to get into and out of. He did not greatly mind taking his time, either then or when he was driving towards the Yard. He wanted the notion he had about Cartwright to take root. Coincidence was acceptable up to a point, but the Maybell-Daw coincidence was quite remarkable, and if by any chance

204

Cartwright was picked up near Paddington, it would not be simply remarkable, it would be astonishing.

He was at the Yard at twenty minutes to one.

In an office almost too brightly lit with fluorescent lighting, Lemaitre grinned up at him from a large desk. Lemaitre was a bony, thin-faced man with a big mouth, who smiled often.

"Guess where we found Cartwright," he said.

"Paddington."

"Edgware Road, so you're not far wrong. He was just coming away from a furrier's place with a couple of mink stoles. He and Daw are both waiting downstairs for you. Want any help?"

"Like to sit in with me?" Gideon asked.

"I'd better not, George, there's a lot coming in to-night. Small stuff, mostly, but you know how it is."

"Right," said Gideon. "Who've you got to come and take notes for me?"

"Young Brennison. Remember him, he——"

"I remember him," said Gideon. "The one who's more Irish than you're Cockney."

Brennison was tall and raw-boned, with the look of the Irish about him, but not a very pronounced brogue, and renowned as a shorthand writer. He entered the first waiting room with Gideon, sat in a corner, and took out his pencil and pad; he had a gift of effacing himself so that whoever was questioning a suspect had the field all to himself.

Charlie Daw was a small, hardy, thin man, with a thin mouth and hard blue eyes; he had a greyish pallor, the kind which often comes from many years in prison. There was nothing remotely prepossessing about him, and in his limited way he was a thoroughly evil man.

"So I said I'd get Maybell, and one of these days I would've, but do you think I'd be a bloody fool enough to make it look like murder?" he said to Gideon. "Not on your flicking life. I come out of stir flat broke, and you bloody busies hound me everywhere I go. I had to try and make a living somehow."

"Who put you on to the job tonight?" asked Gideon. "You didn't think that one up for yourself, you haven't been out long enough to case that or any other place properly. Let's have the truth—who told you about the job?"

"You saying some so-and-so squealed on me?"

"You've got a mind. Use it," Gideon said. He was a foot taller and four inches broader than the prisoner, who was standing by a chair, bitter-faced, his fists clenched as if he would like to squeeze the life out of whoever had informed the police. Gideon offered him a cigarette, and he snatched it. "Right," Gideon went on as the man lit it. "Now start thinking. Someone told you that the Hammersmith job was worth doing. Someone told you to do it tonight. Someone killed Maybell tonight. See if you can add up two and two."

Daw was drawing hard at the cigarette.

"Don't make me have to spell it out for you," Gideon said.

"Gawd!" exclaimed Daw, and his eyes blazed with fury. "It was Si Mitchell, the son of a bitch! He told me he'd see me right, said he knew where I could unload the stuff, he even staked me ten quid. Why, if I——"

Cartwright was a man of much higher intelligence than Daw, and he spoke in a well-modulated voice; it was hard to believe that he had taught his only son a life of crime.

"I meant to get Archer all right, and I hope he died, it will save me the trouble. It wasn't Si Mitchell who gave me the key to the furriers, though, but one of Si's boys. You'd better work on them."

"Bring in Simon Mitchell," said the radio, the teletype and the telephone, to every divisional station and every substation of the Metropolitan Police. "He is wanted for questioning in connection with the murder of Sergeant Maybell. Bring in Simon Mitchell . . .

But Mitchell was not found that night.

17

SNATCH

Helen was in the bathroom, and the two men could hear the shower hissing and splashing. Ryman was in a singlet and a pair of flannels; he had not yet shaved. Stone had been up before any of them, and was shaved and spruce, his hair plastered down so that it looked as if it were groomed with a black lacquer paint. There were dark shadows under his eyes, and his movements were jerky as he stared down at the headlines in the three newspapers which had just arrived at the flat.

LONDON HUNT FOR POLICEMAN'S KILLER

ran one, and the sub-heading ran:

Every available London policeman
joins search

TWO POLICEMEN SAVAGELY ATTACKED

ran another.

"We'll get the killers if it's the last thing we do"
—Gideon of the Yard

GREATEST LONDON MANHUNT

said the third simply.

Ryman was beginning to smile as he read these. He glanced at Stone, who did not speak, but was reading the text of the report on Archer.

"God!" he gasped.

"What's that?"

"Archer's alive."

"You bungled it!"

". . . waiting by his bedside," Stone was reading, and he wiped the sweat off his forehead. "They want a statement, so he's not come round, thank God for that. Not that he could say anything if he did talk, he didn't see me."

"You sure?" Ryman demanded.

"Of course I'm sure!"

"Then stop yapping," Ryman said, and his eyes seemed to dart to and fro as he read the story in the *Globe.* "Maybell was dead when they picked him up, I didn't fall down on my part of it." He was reading for something else, flung the paper aside and picked up another. "Anything there about Daw?"

"No."

"Cartwright?"

"No."

"That's all that matters," said Ryman. "They can't get on to us anyhow; even if Si was still in the country they couldn't get on to us, and they can't get on to Si unless Daw or Cartwright is picked up."

Stone said: "You didn't talk like that yesterday."

"I didn't think we'd have Archer alive yesterday."

"What the hell difference does that make?" Stone

209

stared into Ryman's eyes, and began to scowl; and as Ryman glowered at him, Stone moistened his lips and said in a strange, almost whispering voice: "You don't know what you're doing, you've made a hell of a mess of this. I always knew you were too clever, and now——"

He broke off.

They stood glowering, the newspapers on a table between them. Helen came out of the bathroom, wearing a wrap which was painted with huge daffodils. She had on no make-up, her complexion was without a blemish, and a shower cap made her face a perfect oval.

"What's the matter with you two?" she demanded, looking from one to the other.

Stone said: "He's boxed the whole thing up."

"If you——" Ryman began.

"Now, take it easy. Little birdies in their nest mustn't disagree," reproved Helen, and she went to Ryman and took his hand and smiled sweetly at Stone. "All you wanted to do was make that Gideon man and the police busy so that you could handle the bank job without much trouble. Right?"

"Right," agreed Ryman. "And that swine, Gideon——"

"I had just a peep at the newspapers and I should say the cops are going to be very busy," Helen said. "So what are you worrying about? The only one who might be able to put a finger on you is Si Mitchell, and he's in France. We've just got to keep our heads, and collect that baby; then we'll be right on top. And I'm going to drive the kid away—no one will look twice, then. There's no need for me to be at the bungalow." She gave Ryman a little push, and asked: "Do you want me to get you cornflakes and milk, or shall we send down to the restaurant for a real breakfast? *I'm* hungry."

Three hundred yards away, Mrs. Mountbaron was looking in at the nursery, where the baby gazed up at her, and then gave a quick, almost convulsive smile; its hands began to wave with sudden eagerness.

Gideon read the newspapers as he ate a hurried breakfast, a little after nine o'clock; he had not reached home until four, and had had exactly four and a half hours' sleep. Kate was the brisk and competent housewife; he could hear bacon sizzling. The reports of the attacks on the police did not greatly interest him, and he searched for the mention of the two arrests, but found none. He had asked that no mention be made of the arrests and the newspapers were being helpful. There were diverse comments, including letters in two of the newspapers. One said:

We are now finding out the bitter truth of the assertions made by Commander Gideon of Scotland Yard about the deplorable situation in the Metropolitan Police. Whether Commander Gideon was wise to make his statement so publicly is immaterial. The brutal fact is that the greatest police force in the world is in danger of being reduced to impotence . . .

Gideon folded the newspaper, handed it to Kate as she put his breakfast in front of him, folded another paper to a column headed: *Crisis at the Yard*, and read:

An axe can be a two-edged weapon. The economy axe which is being held like a sword of Gideon, if we may be allowed a metaphor, is most certainly

211

two-edged where the Metropolitan Police force is concerned. It may save the taxpayer a few hundred thousand pounds, but it will certainly cost him much more as a private citizen.

Sooner or later, the brutal savagery of such crimes as those committed last night will bring this home to the authorities, who can hardly have forgotten the two weeks' old murder of another detective who was carrying out his duty.

Gideon read that between mouthfuls of sausage, bacon and egg, and saw that Kate had finished the other leading article. He put his newspaper down, and picked up his teacup. Kate had only done her hair roughly, and hadn't made-up, but her eyes were as bright as ever.

"I don't know whether you're going to win," she said, "but I'm beginning to feel sure that you're not going to lose."

She was just about on the mark, Gideon thought, hopefully. He picked up the receiver of the downstairs telephone, asked for the Yard, and inquired about David Archer. "No change," he called out to Kate. "I'll try not to be late, dear." He hurried out to his car, passing two neighbours on the way, each anxious to stop and have a word, each making a point of using the title Commander. He drove more quickly now than he had during the night. The Yard was a different picture altogether; dozens of men were on the move, there was much briskness and bustle—not really unusual, but not quite typical. He caught the prevailing excitement, which stimulated him as it would nearly every man here. He hurried to the lift, eager to find if there was anything new in. Men saluted, nodded, smiled, and called out greetings. He thrust open the door of his own office, and four men glanced round at him.

Bell was there, looking chubby and very bright-eyed; Sergeant Culverson was big and rather like a good-natured bear. Lemaitre hadn't gone home, but looked as if he could fall asleep on his feet.

And Scott-Marle was standing with his back to the window: it was the first time Gideon had ever seen him in this office.

"Good morning, sir. 'Morning all." Gideon hardly knew whether to be pleased or sorry that the Old Man was present; it might stifle informality. But it did not seem to have affected the others yet, and Lemaitre said:

" 'Morning, George. Glad some people have got time to sleep."

A telephone bell rang, and Bell answered it.

Gideon joined the Commissioner.

"Anything I can do for you, sir?"

"Came to see you, and found the others coping," said Scott-Marle. He looked pale and thin-cheeked, was a little thin-voiced, too; judged from his appearance and manner now, he was a man without enthusiasm or strong feeling. "You don't know that Superintendent Lemaitre discovered that his man Mitchell flew to Paris yesterday, did you?"

"Sure?" Gideon flashed to Lemaitre.

"No doubt about it this time," Lemaitre said, with deep satisfaction. "A flash came in just after you left, didn't think there was any need to keep you out of bed any longer. I happened to know that Lodwick's in Paris on that currency job, he went over again yesterday morning, so I asked him to have a word with the Sûreté. They traced Mitchell for us, and Lodwick's bringing him over. They're due at London Airport at ten o'clock. That might be a call from the airport to say they've got in."

"Well, I think I'll go back to bed," Gideon said.

"Things get done when I'm not here. Did Mitchell come willingly?"

"Apparently. There was no time to get an extradition order, anyhow. Not much doubt about the facts now, George." Lemaitre had the gift of being completely natural, whatever the circumstances. "Mitchell put Daw and Cartwright up to the jobs they did, and there isn't much doubt they were to be framed for the attacks on our chaps."

"I'd like to know what's behind it," Gideon said. He felt a little out of place, without having his chair to go to, and with Scott-Marle also standing. "No point in anyone without a grudge wanting to kill a couple of our fellows for the sake of it, and you can be sure there's a pretty big reason for it." He rubbed his chin. Bell had finished on the telephone, and was making a note; so it wasn't very important, just the inevitable reports coming in. "Been thinking about that since I got up," Gideon said to Scott-Marle. "It was pretty obvious that there was a big motive. Only one thing I can think of."

"Damned if I can think of one," interpolated Lemaitre.

Bell asked: "Have you got something?"

Scott-Marle was looking at Gideon with a curiously intense smile; as if he was really stirred at last.

"What is it?" he asked.

"The idea is to draw us off," said Gideon. "We've got to take the rough with the smooth, and some of the rough about the publicity I've been getting is that everyone knows how tight we're stretched. Wouldn't put it past someone to toss a couple of smoke bombs, metaphorically speaking, so as to get us on one foot. If that's what's happening, then biggish things might be planned. These chaps would be pretty sure that we'd be kept so busy today that it would seem the best time." He turned to Scott-Marle. "You agree, sir?"

"You're the detective," the Commissioner said. "It certainly makes sense to me."

"What've we got?" Lemaitre demanded, rubbing his eyes. "What happens Friday? Any bullion movement out to the docks or the airports? Any special movement of jewels? Any——"

"Joe, get the file marked 'Friday' out of my right-hand drawer," said Gideon. "No, never mind, I'll get it." He hurried across, and as Bell opened the drawer, took the necessary file out, slapped it on the desk, and opened it. "This was planned down to the last dot," he said, "and that means they're after something that happens every Friday, or else something we've had plenty of notice about for today." He found that Scott-Marle had moved with him; all except Culverson, who was watching from the small desk, crowded round him. "Morely's auction," he read. "Movement of bullion to and from the Bank of England from these points." He pointed with a pencil at a map. "Small consignments and all very strongly protected, I wouldn't think anyone would have a cut at those. Geramino's jewel auction is every Friday. The post office carries a lot of soiled notes from most of the provincial banks to the bank of England, it's clearance day. Hmm." He stared at the details about the soiled notes. "If that's it, the problem is to know where to start. There are four main collecting centres in the City, and all the money is sent out to the destruction plant in one van *from* the Bank of England. Always did think it should be destroyed at the Bank, but ——"

He broke off.

"Can't take anything for granted, but I wouldn't mind putting my money on a used notes job," Lemaitre said softly. "Hasn't been tried for five or six years. Up to a hundred thousand quid for the taking. What are you going to do, George?"

Bell and the others were asking the same question, silently.

Gideon said: "I'm going to draw a dozen men from each of the Divisions which can spare them, and protect all the banks concerned in this. And I'm going to have a special guard on all the other vulnerable places, like Morely's, Geramino's, the main post offices and the big banks. If they raid a bank or go for any of these places and we haven't taken precautions, we'd kick ourselves." He had almost forgotten that the Commissioner was present. "Wonder if Mitchell's on his way yet."

The telephone bell rang almost on his words; the sergeant lifted the receiver, and a moment later said:

"Yes, sir, he's just leaving London Airport. Should be here in half an hour, and if he knows anything——" he broke off. "Mr. Lodwick and Mr. Chappel are with him."

"Thanks," said Gideon, and dropped into the chair which Bell had vacated, picked up another telephone and said: "Gimme Information." He waited only for a moment. "Vic, connect me with the car Lodwick and Chappel are in, somewhere out at London Airport . . . Yes, I'll hold on." He looked into Scott-Marle's eyes now. "If Mitchell's come willingly he might have decided to turn Queen's evidence, no reason why he shouldn't be questioned on the way here . . . Hallo, that you, Chappel? . . . Lodwick, yes, you'll do. Now try to find out from Mitchell . . ."

"Don't think I'm nagging, Mrs. Mountbaron said, "but do be careful crossing Park Lane, Nanny. I always hold my breath while I see you cross, the cars come so fast."

"Clarissa won't come to any harm with me," the girl

216

assured her, and smiled. "Don't worry, ma'am. I'd rather get run over myself."

"I really think you would," said Mrs. Mountbaron. She bent down, kissed Clarissa's forehead, and then opened the door to the passage. The Nanny pushed the perambulator out into the passage and along towards the lift. Mrs. Mountbaron busied herself for three or four minutes and then, unable to keep away, she went to the window; Nanny should be downstairs by now.

Helen sat in the small saloon car, near the side street along which the nursemaid would come. The car was grey, there were thousands of identical models in London, and the registration number plates would change at the touch of a switch. The rear door was already open an inch, it had only to be given a single pull to open it wide. Stone was standing near the corner, and Ryman was in his own car on the other side of the street.

The nursemaid came wheeling her charge in a pink and white perambulator with a pink and white hood, to keep the sun out of its eyes. The nursemaid, rather thin and not particularly attractive, was pushing the pram steadily and bending forward, making chuckling noises at the child. She did not notice Stone at the corner, although he was only ten yards away. She did not see the car as it started off noisily; and suddenly she stopped pushing, for the car came straight across the road towards her, and for a moment it looked as if it would mount the pavement.

". . . fool!" she snapped. "Why don't you ——"

She broke off, as the car stopped. The driver, with an eye-mask covering the top of his face, sprang out of it so swiftly that she had no time to shout. He struck her viciously on the back of the head. As he did so, she was just aware of another man racing from the corner.

She tried to scream.

She felt another sharp blow, and staggered, letting the pram go and gasping for breath, terror deep in her.

She did not see the man snatch the baby from the perambulator and go racing to the corner, carrying it as he would a rugby football. She was collapsing as the car drove off. She did not hear the second car, round the corner, as it started towards Park Lane, with the baby lying on the back seat, looking up at its own pink fingers.

Stone squeezed into Ryman's car while it was moving. He saw a man some distance away, and a taxi approaching the main entrance to the block of flats; that was all.

"We've done it," Ryman said, in a hoarse voice. "What did I tell you, we've done it. All we've got to do is go back to my place, treat ourselves to a drink, and then get ready for the afternoon job. Helen will give us a ring when she gets to the cottage." He was grinning excitedly as he swung round the next two corners, and drew up quite near the block where he had his own flat. He and Stone had been away for twenty minutes in all; it was as easy as that. He parked the car, and went striding along, shoulders back, handsome and devil-may-care looking, with Stone less assured by his side. As they turned into the main entrance, a car moved behind them, and two big men stepped from the entrance lobby.

There was a moment's horrified pause, then:

"The *police*," Stone gasped.

"Keep your head," Ryman said savagely, and he managed to keep up a semblance of a smile. "Want me?" he asked the nearer man.

"Are you Keith Ryman?"

"I am. What business is it ——"

"I am a police officer, and it is my duty to charge you with complicity in the murder of Police Sergeant Herbert Maybell on the night of . . ." the man began.

Ryman swung round.

Stone was standing absolutely still, a little polished dummy of a man. Two more cars had drawn up, there was a ring of policemen and detectives; and neither Ryman nor Stone even had a chance to run.

There was Mrs. Mountbaron, panic-stricken; the nursemaid in an ambulance on the way to hospital; the police, watching every danger-point of Gideon's Friday list. There was Helen driving the little Austin along towards Barnes, snatching a glance over her shoulder every time she was forced to stop at lights, to see that the child was all right. She reached the riverside cottage in three-quarters of an hour, quite sure she was safe. But as she drew up, men appeared at the sides of the cottage and others appeared from the far side of the road. Before she could utter a word, the car was surrounded.

"Child safe and unhurt," Gideon said, rubbing his empty pipe with his big thumb. "Both men and woman in the lock-up." He used terms like 'lock-up' when he was in an expansive mood. "Stone's ready to talk, like Mitchell; it looks as if the only real dangerous man was Ryman. Neither he nor Stone has a record. It's time we put that right."

The Commissioner, now with Gideon in the Assistant Commissioner's office, was looking at him with his head on one side, and that almost unwilling smile on his lips.

"You forget that Stone informed us that the soiled treasury note van was the key objective."

"I didn't forget," said Gideon, and looked at the Commissioner thoughtfully, then went on: "Mind if I say something blunt?" Scott-Marle nodded. "Whenever we get wind of something like today's job, we're on a sound thing. We've got every trick any crook ever tried down on our list, and I'm lucky, because I've got a good memory. I know most of them by heart. But I'm only one of hundreds, the job starts down on the beat. Every man in uniform knows the weaknesses and the strength of people of his own streets. He knows the householders who always leave windows open, the people who leave keys dangling on a piece of string at the letterbox, the people who leave a key under the front-door mat, the shopkeeper who hasn't troubled to buy a safe—he knows the lot. He has to. And what he knows is passed on to the CID in his Division. They all know the most vulnerable houses and shops worth breaking into, the men in their manor most likely to do a certain job. It goes up from them to the Divisional DDIs and upwards. Our chaps know the Metropolitan area so well no one would believe it if they didn't have the evidence before their eyes. I just happen to be at the top of all the Divisions, but I came up through all the others. The general knowledge, the tricks, the—the expertise of these chaps is the nearest thing to a living miracle I'll ever see."

He stopped, and grinned a little shamefacedly.

The Commissioner said: "Rogerson always told me that you knew more about your job than any man he'd ever met, and I can see what he meant. One thing I can tell you will cheer you up. I had a call to the Home Office this morning. The Minister told me that it was decided at yesterday's cabinet not to force any economies on any of us here. That's confidential, of course, you know how these fellows hate admitting that they're wrong. The thing which will please you most, though, is that the Home Secretary promised me that he would do battle with the Treasury to get our grant up. Now you've really got something to get your teeth into."

"They say," said Popple to Gideon, "that the Old Man told the Home Sec. that if they forced any economies on to the Force, he'd resign and tell the reason why. Almost a pity he didn't have to."

"Wouldn't surprise me if that's right," mused Gideon. "Like to do something for me from now on?"

"Just name it."

"Keep my name out of the newspapers."

Popple grinned.

Gideon saw the newspapers, with all their huge headlines, photographs of the Mountbaron baby, the three persons charged, the whole story; a positive surfeit of news. But there was no word about the soiled notes plot, and there was only a passing mention of George Gideon. That suited him very well. When he went into the living-room, Kate looked up, saw his expression, and knew that he was in a contented mood.

"Get yourself a whisky and soda," she said, "and I'll get your dinner. Any news?"

"We not only haven't lost," Gideon told her, "there's just a chance that we'll win."

MASTERWORKS OF MYSTERY
BY MARY ROBERTS RINEHART!

THE YELLOW ROOM   (2262, $3.50)
The somewhat charred corpse unceremoniously stored in
the linen closet of Carol Spencer's Maine summer home set
the plucky amateur sleuth on the trail of a killer. But each
step closer to a solution led Carol closer to her own immi-
nent demise!

THE CASE OF JENNIE BRICE   (2193, $2.95)
The bloodstained rope, the broken knife—plus the disap-
pearance of lovely Jennie Brice—were enough to convince
Mrs. Pittman that murder had been committed in her
boarding house. And if the police couldn't see what was in
front of their noses, then the inquisitive landlady would just
have to take matters into her own hands!

THE GREAT MISTAKE   (2122, $3.50)
Patricia Abbott never planned to fall in love with wealthy
Tony Wainwright, especially after she found out about the
wife he'd never bothered to mention. But suddenly she was
trapped in an extra-marital affair that was shadowed by un-
spoken fear and shrouded in cold, calculating murder!

THE RED LAMP   (2017, $3.50)
The ghost of Uncle Horace was getting frisky—turning on
lamps, putting in shadowy appearances in photographs.
But the mysterious nightly slaughter of local sheep seemed
to indicate that either Uncle Horace had developed a bizarre
taste for lamb chops . . . or someone was manipulating appearances with a deadly sinister purpose!

A LIGHT IN THE WINDOW   (1952, $3.50)
Ricky Wayne felt uncomfortable about moving in with her
new husband's well-heeled family while he was overseas
fighting the Germans. But she never imagined the depths of
her in-laws' hatred—or the murderous lengths to which they
would go to break up her marriage!

*Available wherever paperbacks are sold, or order direct from the
Publisher. Send cover price plus 50¢ per copy for mailing and handling to Zebra Books, Dept. 2797, 475 Park Avenue South, New
York, N.Y. 10016. Residents of New York, New Jersey and Penn-
sylvania must include sales tax. DO NOT SEND CASH.*